Scribe Publications
TWO NOVELLAS

David Vogel was born in 1891 in Satanov, Podolia (now Ukraine), and when World War I broke out he was living in Vienna, where he was arrested as an enemy alien. He emigrated to Tel Aviv in 1929, but left for Berlin after a year, and later settled in Paris. After the outbreak of World War II, he was imprisoned by the French as an Austrian citizen, and later by the Nazis as a Jew. In 1944, he was deported to Auschwitz, where he perished.

TWO NOVELLAS

IN THE SANATORIUM
& FACING THE SEA

DAVID VOGEL

Translated by Philip Simpson and Daniel Silverstone

SCRIBE
Melbourne • London

Scribe Publications Pty Ltd

18–20 Edward St, Brunswick, Victoria 3056, Australia
50A Kingsway Place, Sans Walk, London, EC1R 0LU, United Kingdom

Published by Scribe 2013

Typeset in 12/16 pt Dante MT by the publishers
Printed and bound in China by 1010 Printing

A Cataloguing-in-Publication data record for this book is available from the
National Library of Australia

scribepublications.com.au
scribepublications.co.uk

CONTENTS

IN THE
SANATORIUM

'Ah, Ornik!'

'Good morning, Ornik!'

'How's your temperature?'

'And the phlegm count?'

On the open balcony of the first floor, most of the patients were already reclining on the white iron benches, set side by side along the whole length of the narrow balcony. They lay supine, wrapped in folded blankets up to their noses, to ward off the transparent, searing chill of a winter morning.

Like a huge and heavy machine, Irma Ornik, business-school graduate, propelled his gigantic body slowly, movement after movement, the few paces between his room and the bench. His broad, slightly rounded shoulders slanted obliquely from right to left; and planted in the middle, without any sign of a neck, was a great head as round as a pumpkin.

The gibes of his friends bounced off his big body like rubber bullets. Ornik did not reply, but smiled to himself and muttered something, while his large hairy hands — protruding from the elbows out of the short sleeves of his tattered dressing-gown, which Ornik only used now for lying down — adjusted the setting of the bench with slow, measured movements.

Then, with great care, Ornik deposited his eighty-six

kilograms on the bench and wrapped himself thoroughly in the blankets until only his massive head was visible, wearing a stiff woollen hat, mountaineer-style.

Above the mountain ridges to the left, their crags capped with blue snow, a long strip of sky was reddening steadily. In the open expanse of the sky a little white cloud drifted, turning pink on one side. As for the chain of hills to the right, a smidgen of vibrant colour was now infused into the dark bronze of their high diagonal. A larger moon than usual was impaled on the western heights, an alien, superfluous moon, all pallid, reminiscent of a forgotten streetlamp still burning in the morning.

Ornik lay for some time without moving and gazed out at Mendel Ridge, which sealed in the blue distance the aperture of the long Albano Valley. Suddenly he felt a kind of bubble rising from his chest to his throat. Ornik removed his right hand from under the blankets and reached for the flat spittoon on the chair beside the bed, opened the nickel cover with his thumb, raised his head a little, and hawked into it, emitting a muffled sound. When he had finished he looked with one eye, closing the other, inside the spittoon, examining it as if he were an expert, until he noticed filaments of blood in the green gunge, like the veins in the white of an inflamed eye. At once Ornik felt painful exhaustion spreading gradually from his back and extending to his knees, setting them shaking. He closed the receptacle, shook it, studied the contents for a moment through the blue glass, and put it back in its place.

Then Ornik took two thermometers from the chair,

one of them in a sheath of nickel and the other in a sheath of red paper; unpacked them from the sheaths, which he left on the blanket; inserted the thermometers, one under his armpit and the other in his mouth, for greater accuracy; and peered at his watch.

'Again? Didn't you take your temperature just now?' said Ornik's room-mate, Seberg the engineer, lying on the next bench.

After twenty minutes — Ornik did not measure things for ten minutes but for twenty, to avoid the likelihood of error — he took out the thermometers one after the other and compared the results: 37.4 degrees, again! And a sharp pain stabbed at his temples.

When the sun's rays began to invade the eyes, the four balconies of the 'sanatorium for the needy' came to life. Everyone was in good spirits, as lying down became comfortable and even rather pleasant. Conversations began; benches were dragged noisily across the floor. Those who were forbidden the sun lowered the folding curtains attached to the walls and stretched them out to form slanting roofs, and beside these Irma Ornik erected a great grey booth resembling a market stall — no one knew how he had got his hands on it.

From the women's balconies above, the sharp voice of Trudi Wizel, the little devil from Prague, called to Frau Schnabel, who wasn't supposed to lie down until the sun came out. 'Frau Schnabel, she's still asleep!'

'Who's asleep?' asked a muffled voice.

'The sun!'

A clever idea occurred to Adolf Ritter, lying in the

middle of the balcony. Pointing first to right and left, he gave his instructions while slightly raising the upper part of his body, commanding in a restrained voice and with helpful gestures, like a general in battle already thrown from his horse: 'One-two-the-ree!'

And all the residents of the first floor shouted in unison, 'Frau Schna-bel — the su-un!'

From above came a strident gale of laughter from many female mouths. Soon after this, for some reason, Lyuba Goldis, the Russian student, shouted at Trudi Wizel, denouncing her fragile but affable friend: 'Trudi's a goat!'

And Trudi answered, 'And you're a Russian goat!' to the laughter of the rest of the girls. Adolf Ritter gave the order again, and from a dozen mouths leaped the nickname by which Lyuba Goldis always called the overweight Richard Berlin: 'Big bad black boy!'

'Stupid ox!' Lyuba shouted down with a laugh.

Doctor Macleese came round 'to pay visits'. With his head tilted back and his chest puffed up, he paced in his white coat along the balcony, while Sister Lisl, a short, shrivelled Tyrolean, dogged his footsteps. By every bench Doctor Macleese asked questions, always in the same indifferent tone and with the same words — 'What's the situation?' 'Temperature?' 'Bowel movements?' — while casting an eye over the temperature chart held out to him by the patient, and adjusting the medication for this one or the other, all recorded by Sister Lisl in her little notebook.

In an almost inaudible whisper, which had been his habit this last year and a half 'to avoid straining the lung', Ornik laid his complaints before Doctor Macleese, who smiled with his thick-lipped mouth, exposing big yellow teeth like those of a horse. Ornik recounted his symptoms in detail, and his round face with its turbid pallor did not move at all.

'Last night it was insomnia, Herr Doktor, until three or four in the morning, then fitful sleep and sweating. Yesterday evening a pain in the back, on the upper right side, about the size of a krone, from eight until nine. Lots of phlegm, with traces of blood, and this morning the temperature is already 37.4. Tinnitus in the left ear, headaches, stabbing pains in the chest near the heart.'

'Nothing to worry about there, Ornik,' Doctor Macleese assured him, 'no danger at all.' And to Sister Lisl, standing behind him, 'Bromine alkali. Smear iodine on the painful places before sleep. In the evening, poultices.'

What does he *know!* thought Ornik scornfully. *Doctor Kalbol — if only* he *were here!*

But Doctor Kalbol, the only doctor whom Ornik trusted, was in Vienna, and Ornik had to be content with sending him a long and detailed letter once a fortnight on the progress of his illness, enclosing a temperature chart that he drew up especially for him.

Meanwhile, Betty was already doing the rounds with second breakfasts: always the same glass of tasteless milk, and the same two slices of bread and butter, already repellent.

'And where is the bacon, Frau Betty?' asked Karl Levy playfully, a blond Viennese boy whose puffy face was permanently red.

'In the shop!' The maid laughed.

The invalids sat on the benches and chewed. Some of them furtively took slices of sausage from under their mattresses, looked around, and stuffed them hurriedly into their mouths. Ornik ate without appetite, chewing repeatedly for the sake of good digestion.

But the sun was already a substantial distance from the dazzling, snowy crags, and was flooding the Albano Valley with a yellow, dry warmth. The vineyards on the plain bowed down, listless. The vines were scattered close to the ground like a tangle of insignificant roots, and the poles planted next to them now seemed dry and utterly superfluous, entwined together like bleached skeletons. The unsealed road wound behind trees and gardens. Opposite, some distance away, the low, clean houses of the Untermais brightened peacefully. And from amid the cluster of houses and the smart hotels with green shutters on the slope, below the ridge of hills to the left, as if one were perching on the roof of another, chequered by the green of trees and bushes, the spires of old, dusty churches reared up here and there, a brief reminder of cloistered reverence in a dim, cool space that reeked of mouldy incense. The mountains were closer now, seeming only a few paces away.

In this tranquillity the inmates sometimes forgot why they were here. Flickering before their eyes were the white summer dresses of young women and their exposed, sunburned arms. The bench became suddenly hard, and the half-hour before the morning walk dragged on endlessly.

Finally the tram returned from its thirty-minute journey to the village of Lana, travelling along with a cacophony of rattling and scraping as it passed close by the sanatorium. Karl Levy was the first to leap from the bench and start folding the blankets.

'Another five minutes yet, Herr Levy!' Sister Lisl yelled in her cracked voice, popping up in the doorway to one of the rooms.

'I must go to …' he lied. And in a whisper: 'Bugger off!'

The patients hurried to get up. Ornik was the only one left lying there. He did not go out for walks, for fear of suffering a stroke.

The room of Adolf Ritter and Sebag Adler in the middle of the first floor was flooded by the lavish brightness of the sun. The room's white walls and the few essential furnishings intensified the light to a blinding pitch.

Before the glass door that was open to the balcony, Ritter stood in his underwear, swabbing his face with eau de cologne, periodically squeezing out drops from the flat bottle in his broad hand. Then he glanced at the mirror above the white enamel washstand and exclaimed with satisfaction, 'My face is already nicely tanned! In the afternoon it will be thirty degrees. Excellent sunshine.'

While inserting his foot, short and clumsy as a block of wood, into a freshly ironed pair of trousers with a razor-sharp crease, Ritter turned his screwed-up myopic eyes to Adler, who was also busy dressing, and continued: 'I need to send a letter to my old man, to get him to send me some money. And get him to extend my leave of absence. The other clerks will die of jealousy! Ha-ha — every year I go away for two months, and they just get one month off. And

I have to apply again to the health department and get a letter of endorsement from that monkey-doctor Macleese.

'Herr Adler' — Ritter turned, mid-conversation, to a new topic — 'is it by any chance your intention to join us for a walk? A small group of a few couples. Berlin will bring the camera with him and we'll all have our picture taken.'

'No!'

'Why not? Invite some girl, you know —' A wonderful idea popped up in Ritter's head. 'Invite Marishka Cohen.' His dwarfish and overfed body melted in excitement. 'What a girl! She knows what boys were made for. She's not one of the worst looking either, although she isn't in the first bloom of youth. I've had my eye on her for some time, and she doesn't object; in the dining room she always turns her lorgnette to me ... But, you know, Trudi is such a nuisance. I feel sorry for that girl. Yesterday she cried all the way through supper again, and didn't eat anything. The girl isn't looking after herself at all, either crying, or acting the devil.

'Ah!' Ritter remembered whom they had been discussing, after a moment. 'If only I'd met her in Vienna, this Marishka ... but she's not getting away this time, you mark my words.'

In the meantime he had already finished dressing. Everything was as it should be: the collar white and clean, the bowtie. But the sides of his long, thick nose were turning redder than usual on account of swollen glands in his mouth and throat, and Ritter felt around the affected area and remembered he ought to take a clean handkerchief.

'Well, are you coming with us?' Ritter changed his question.

Adler shook his head.

They both went down in their felt slippers to the boot room on the floor below. On the polished stone staircase a group of girls, talking and laughing, caught up with them, including the thin, volatile Trudi Wizel in her cloak and bottle-green hat.

'*At your service, Trudi my dear! How are you today? Temperature?*' Ritter said, imitating Doctor Macleese.

Trudi held out her narrow hands to the two youths and said gaily, 'What conspiracy are you cooking up now, fine pair that you are?'

Almost the entire space of the boot room was occupied by a tall iron cage in the middle, made up of row upon row of little square compartments where the patients' shoes were stored between walks. The men's were kept on the right and the women's on the left — well cleaned, of full and half height, of all shapes and styles. Now the patients crowded the narrow space next to the cage, some of them standing on one leg, leaning against the wall, and sweatily tying the laces for the other foot; and some of them waiting patiently in the corridor.

In the corner of the heaving boot room stood Herr Kisch, heavily shod, standing short as if truncated, his lugubrious lips parted in a lustful smile. In his modulated voice Herr Kisch addressed his remarks, which sounded as if they came from a mouth full of spittle, to Greta Finger, who stood opposite him, bent down and busy putting on a brown boot. He said, just for the sake of saying something,

'And how is she today, Fräulein Finger? Which way will she go? And who will have the privilege of enjoying her company?'

'Why, you, Herr Kisch, I shall be with you, my dear! To the ends of the earth and the end of time.' Greta Finger laughed.

'How delightful, Fräulein — and what a great honour for me.'

When he laughed, the little red eyes of Herr Kisch contracted and disappeared completely amid the wrinkles of his forty years. The only features visible were his sharp nose and thick black moustache, trimmed in the English style, and the stiff bristles that covered his face from his jaws to his eyes, and that had not been shaved for some days.

Herr Kisch looked with excitement at Greta Finger's leg, an attractive and shapely leg in a light stocking, and he said in a thick voice, 'I find that her face is not yet perfect, Fräulein Finger. She has to eat a lot, madame, I say, eat a lot and put on some weight. She's beautiful, of course, even more than that, pretty I should say, but the lung … for the sake of the lung …'

'I shall try, Herr Kisch, of course.'

'Herr Adler' — Kisch turned to him — 'perhaps you'll be kind enough to give me another cigarette. Mine have run out; I'll buy some later and reimburse you. You've had four of mine already …'

'Take a cigarette, Herr Kisch!'

Standing squarely in the long, dark corridor was Fräulein Han, the superintendent, a forty-five-year-old virgin, in a white apron with a big bunch of keys hanging from it. As she spoke to one of the assistants, her detective's eyes, small and sharp, glanced from time to time towards the boot room, and all her attention was devoted to what was going on there.

Everywhere you meet that bitch! thought Adler, and he greeted her as he passed.

When he left the garden that surrounded the sanatorium, he lit himself a cigarette and inhaled the smoke greedily, after many hours of not smoking. The pungent smoke wheezed in his damaged lung and caused him palpable exhaustion, but Adler didn't notice this. He pondered for a while and unfastened the buttons of his overcoat with a sense of liberation.

On the grey foundation under the iron fence of the Hotel Continental garden, a number of lizards were warming themselves in the sunlight, looking from a distance like elongated green stains. When Adler passed by them, they silently took flight into the dense vegetation inside the garden.

The waters of the Passer, green and smoothest at this wintry hour, roared and rumbled in the deep channel, sometimes in the centre and sometimes to the side, bypassing the big outcrops of rock powdered with white dust, splitting sometimes into two narrow jets and reuniting again a little further on. There was a revelation here of powerful forces, fighting with all their might for their survival. Adler was filled with hope. His diseased lung was sure to be cured, and all would be well again. He suddenly felt absolutely healthy.

The promenade along the edge of the river was full of activity. Thin, lanky English ladies swayed with their clumsy gait, dragging their pedigree dogs behind them, cameras slung at their sides. Their colourful anoraks and large sunglasses, which hid most of their faces, fed the imagination with fragments of pictures of other lives, distant and strange lives that one might have read about in some book. Italian officers, mostly of short stature and with tanned and lined faces, strolled around like lords of the manor, sure of their worth. Their black or red capes, which were broader around the base, turned them into miniature mobile pyramids.

But many of the pedestrians were pale and lean, stooped and leaning on crutches as they walked, coughing from time to time and clutching their chests with their hands, feverish eyes scouring for vacant seats on the benches to the side. Porters in red service caps pushed three-wheeled carriages carrying invalids with despondent faces, as yellow as parchment, wrapped in woollen flowery blankets.

In one of these carriages sat a girl of about eighteen, pale and thin. A middle-aged woman, tall and slightly clumsy, the watery colour of her face suggesting that she was from the north, walked beside the carriage. Without any conscious intention, Adler found himself walking close to her, and occasionally glanced furtively at the girl's blue eyes and her sickly hand with its taut veins, resting listlessly on the blanket. 'This is definitely the mother.' Adler forced himself to restrain the unpleasant feeling that was beginning to spread within him and take over the whole of his interior. 'Definitely the mother, a good mother. There is even some similarity between the two women's faces, a strong similarity, you could say ...' But Adler's former hope was no longer in him. Suddenly he saw himself transported in such a carriage and immediately felt a sense of fatigue in all his limbs, and sweat poured down his back. Ech! He tried to shake it off and to remove himself, taking hasty steps to the other side of the road.

Near the veranda of the casino, a white building with a big dome, he noticed Rachel Portugal in the distance, approaching with measured gait the round pavilion where a band was playing. Adler changed his direction, with the aim of encountering the girl by chance. After greeting her he said, 'If the lady permits, this gentleman will accompany her for a while.'

A twitch of hesitation showed at the corner of the girl's mouth. She wanted to go on further. She stopped for a moment, turned on him her black, penetrating eyes from under narrow brows curved like bows, and said with a smile: 'Well — if it won't be too boring ...'

'No, of this I can't be at all sure ... It's very possible that one of us will be bored ...'

Rachel Portugal tried to put things right. 'This wasn't what I meant to say, if you'll excuse me! Perhaps we should get out of this crowd, the band's programme today isn't that good.' No, she was referring to something completely different. He should know that not long ago she happened to be accompanied by a certain doctor, a philosopher. He immediately began showing her all the contents of his extensive library. It was a wonderful day, like today, and he pelted her with lofty topics for a whole hour — she hadn't yet recovered from that trip.

'And you're afraid of an "extensive library" with me too, eh? Is there some sign of this in my nose?' Adler joked and pointed to his straight nose.

'No, really!' The girl turned her laughing face towards Adler. 'You must forgive me for not understanding this at once. I forgot to look at his nose ...'

Without noticing it they had walked the full length of the promenade and were now on the Tappeinerweg, which curled and climbed up the slope beside the deep gully of the Passer, amid the green, pungent plants of the south.

'Perhaps we should sit for a while,' suggested Rachel Portugal.

They sat down on a bench on the side of the hill. On the path, shaded by the trees and the abundant bushes, there were nevertheless scattered patches of quivering sunlight, their ownership disputed by large flies with gleaming purple bodies. From the valley rose the endless sound of a waterfall surging, nearby but hidden, and on the opposite side white houses were dotted here and there, clinging to the other slope of the hill, where the San Zeno Castle teetered on the edge: a grey stone castle with its tall, square tower already collapsing.

Adler felt himself suddenly swamped by a flood of pleasure. He glanced at Rachel Portugal, sitting beside him, whose full, capricious mouth, in a pale oval face, now smiled the forgotten serene smile of a baby, and he said, 'Isn't it strange, Fräulein Portugal, that you've travelled such a long way, from India to the Albano Valley, perhaps just to be sitting with me now on this bench?'

'From India, not Hamburg?' The girl chuckled.

'No, only by way of Hamburg. From around Bombay.'

In the distance the tower-clock chimed twelve — it was time to get back.

The promenade was already half empty. The band played the last piece, a Viennese operetta, which seemed strange and slightly absurd amid the brooding mountains all around. The sun beat down vigorously, and Adler took off his hat from time to time and used a handkerchief to wipe away rivulets of sweat from his domed forehead. While walking quickly he muttered, 'Doctor Macleese is bound to be lying in wait in the corridor.'

On every side the invalids started coming together, by themselves and in groups, and streamed towards the tall brick building that from the front resembled a red barracks block.

Adler felt a resurgence of that vague, persistent depression that had taken root since the day he came here. He went with Rachel Portugal into the spacious, well-lit lobby, its two walls covered from top to bottom with big ivory panels. Inscribed on them in big gold letters, line after line, were the names of the founders, presidents, deputies, and all the other persons of note: *Dr Bernard Volk from Prague, President*; *Privy Councillor Dr Mandelstam from Vienna, Founder*; *Benefactress Dame Henrietta Cohen from Austria*; etc. etc.

As always, when he was crossing the lobby, that troublesome verse began weighing on Adler like a heavy ingot — *For such is the way of all mankind* — from which he had to struggle to distance himself for a long time afterwards.

Outside the crowded boot-room he parted from Rachel Portugal. She smiled at him and said, 'Well, time to go back to the harem.'

On the balcony flooded by sunlight, the patients were standing and sitting, thermometers stuck like cigarettes into their mouths. Some of them stood close to the balustrade and leaned their backs against it, looking up and exchanging banter with the girls leaning over the upper balconies.

Richard Berlin was busy drying some photograph prints, spread out on a bench in the sun. The pictures were still damp and black, with no discernible shapes in them. He approached the balustrade and called out anxiously to Lyuba Goldis, 'They haven't come out yet! They need to dry a little longer.'

She laughed at him affectionately, and her slanting eyes flashed green flames. Then she amused herself by dangling her blue scarf down to the first-floor balcony. Adolf Ritter caught it and gave it a tug.

'Hey, let go!' Lyuba yelled, laughing. 'I'm falling down.'

Her trimmed chestnut hair was untidy, divided into two plaits around her lowered head; and through the mesh of the balustrade, appearing for a moment between the flapping wings of her gown, were flashes of white, shapely thigh, between her stockings and her black underwear. The boys narrowed their eyes with a lewd laugh.

Little Windel, Richard Berlin's room-mate, came out in his colourful woollen smoking-jacket, his head tilted towards his left shoulder, which was slightly lower than the other, and his greasy hair plastered to his scalp like some shiny black glue.

Windel said to the gang in his thin, permanently animated voice, 'Lyuba Goldis, it has to be said, is not ugly, but she's too thin. A beanstalk: there's nothing to hold on to! I like a girl with something to hold: a *shiksa* like Missy — she's the business! The grain store and the wine press too!'

As he spoke, his pale narrow cheekbones reddened with emotion, and his eyes, round and prominent as those of a fish, bulged even more.

'And what's your opinion, Herr Adler: am I right?' Windel asked the man towards whom, for some unknown reason, he felt an excess of sympathy.

'You're right, of course.' Adler smiled.

'These charming Jewish girls' — Windel was becoming ever more excited — 'you won't get any pleasure from them, not a hair's breadth ... you might as well take them to the wedding canopy straight away. Today on the promenade I got to know a certain *shiksa* — I'm telling you: beautiful, tip-top! I've already arranged a date at her house; things are going to happen! With me it's always' — Windel tapped two fingers of his right hand on his narrow chest — 'with me it's always one-two-three-GO! But what were you expecting? You think I'm going to stand here and make eyes at the kosher maidens of this leper colony? Abstinence is bad for the lungs: I know that better than sterile old Doctor Volk knows it. After all, I'm from Brigittenau, from the city of Vienna; I don't need a finger to show me the way! A true Viennese knows everything!'

'That's the way it is!' Karl Levy backed him up with good-natured sarcasm. 'I was saying only just now: *Windel knows everything.*'

Meanwhile, inside the building, the dull, quivering notes of the gong were heard. The youths hurried to their lunch. Some of them lingered in the corridor, by the glass door leading to the stairs, and watched the groups of girls coming down from the upper floors. Adler greeted Rachel Portugal, who was passing by with her erect and restrained gait, and she responded with a light nod while a hasty smile passed over her lips. Her somewhat fleshy arms, up to her biceps, protruded from the short sleeves of her blue dress, which exposed semicircles of discoloured chest and back; and her attractive nape was hidden demurely under a lock of her heavy brown hair.

'Rachel Portugal,' said Ritter, 'the most beautiful of all the girls here! A *real* beauty.'

Adler was uneasy. Ritter's remarks about Rachel Portugal aroused an unpleasant kind of sensation in him, for some reason unknown even to him.

'And behind that calm exterior of hers,' Ritter added, 'what a temperament she hides: red hot!'

'Well,' Adler interrupted with a twinge of panic, 'we need to go down.'

In the long dining room, where three long tables took up the entire space, Adler sat at his usual place in the middle of the first table, reserved for men. Opposite him, Herr Kisch was already dipping slices of coarse bread in the steaming soup and taking big gulps, slurping with gusto and great pleasure, as his little eyes contracted and disappeared completely. His face was awash in sweat.

'Eat the soup, Herr Mizel.' With his mouth full, Kisch urged on his neighbour, a Czech youth of about sixteen, seated and eating. 'Eat up, my friend, the soup is excellent today! Believe me.'

'I shall eat, Herr Kisch, with the utmost pleasure,' mocked the young man, narrowing his cunning eyes towards Ritter and Adler.

In the hall, somewhat dark on account of the half-closed shutters, all that was heard for a while was the clicking of a hundred spoons descending and rising in turns, like the pistons of some huge, bizarre machine. One hundred people eating soup. The heat was intense, and many pale faces came out in sickly red blotches. In the doorway leading to the kitchen, the superintendent was seen from time to time, half hidden behind the larder. Her bony face, its swarthy skin stretched tight over it as if on a cobbler's last, showed the persistent malice of ugly women growing old in their virginity. Her sharp little eyes roamed around the room and took everything in — nothing was hidden from them.

Adler fixed his gaze on Ilsa Dohan, sitting opposite him on the central table, with her eyes cast down on the plate before her.

'Your efforts are in vain!' his neighbour, Seberg the engineer, said to him with a smile. 'After the soup her mood will stabilise a little.'

Irma Ornik — who had been in no hurry this time to find a piece of newspaper in his room, to cover his hand when gripping the door handle for reasons of hygiene, as he always did after washing his hands before eating —

came into the dining room now with the hint of a bashful smile on his round, grey face.

'Aa-aa-aaagh!' the group greeted him in strangulated voice.

Between the tables the sweaty serving-maids had already come to gather up the empty plates. A thick racket, a mixture of speech, laughter and the clatter of crockery, drowning in the hot air — which was pressurised even without this. Winks and gestures made their way between people's heads to the girls in the distance, gathered around the third table.

'Have you no sense of shame!' the superintendent suddenly shouted, her face ablaze. 'You're not in the jungle now! How can anyone work in this kind of din? It's enough to drive anyone mad! Like a den of bandits!'

The hubbub ended abruptly, as if cut off with an axe. Filtering through for a moment were the struggles of a stray fly on the windowpane. The silence was oppressive: everyone felt uncomfortable, as if they had been discovered naked in the market in broad daylight.

But very gradually the noise picked up again. First, a few hushed remarks were uttered, and before long the decibels were back at full pitch.

Meanwhile, at the end of the table, a flat oval dish was revealed, and on it a layer of brown beef cutlets, in dry slices. The dish was held out and passed from hand to hand, and meandering in its wake was a tureen containing a pile of golden potatoes, charred at the edges, having been fried for too long.

Kisch was already clutching the fork in his hand, fastening his blazing eyes from a distance on the slices of meat, choosing a fine juicy piece for himself and swallowing his saliva. But when the dish arrived in Karl Levy's hands there was nothing left but two meagre portions, the better of which the latter transferred to his own plate. 'Take another portion, Herr Levy — take it all with a clear conscience!' said Kisch in his low voice.

'How right you are, Herr Kisch!' Levy laughed, taking the last portion, and presenting him with the empty dish.

'Gravy,' said Seberg the engineer to his neighbour, 'please pass the gravy. I can go without anything,' he added, 'except gravy! Without gravy I can't swallow even a morsel.'

Kisch's neighbours chewed with an animated, strident sound, wiping their fingers from time to time on the napkins in their laps before resuming the serious business of mastication, their eyes sparkling and their faces fiery. Everyone helped themselves to a load of potatoes, and Kisch was left with little more than a handful. He sat before a pile of empty plates, which the youths had piled up on purpose, and played with the fork in his hand, full of suppressed anger.

'Bon appetit!' Kisch addressed his neighbours in his quiet voice. 'Potatoes, it seems, aren't cooked properly these days.'

'On the contrary,' said Ritter, who under the table had already loosened the belt of his trousers half a notch, and was now helping himself to the rest of the potatoes in the tureen in front of Kisch. 'On the contrary, as it happens, potatoes are excellent these days.'

'Take it all for yourself, Herr Ritter,' said little Mizel, narrowing his eyes. 'Eat it all with a clear conscience!'

As Kisch's neighbours were about to finish, Paula brought out two cutlets of meat, very small portions, and put one of them on his plate, which he had lifted to her. Kisch went on holding out his plate to Paula — but this portion Paula put on the plate of little Mizel, who had already had some.

'The young man isn't eating much,' said Paula. 'He isn't putting on weight, and the superintendent has told us to pay him a little more attention.'

'But Fräulein Paula,' said Kisch, sounding quiet and re-served while inwardly seething with anger, 'I've not had any potatoes yet, and the meat is cold.'

'I'm sorry, Herr Kisch, we've run out of potatoes. I'll go to the kitchen and see if there are any other vegetables.'

Kisch sliced the meat into tiny pieces, mixing them with spiced cabbage from the full dish that Paula brought him, added the rest of the cold gravy, and started eating.

'This cabbage is very good!' Kisch squeezed out the words from an overfull mouth. 'More agreeable to me than dry, sour potatoes, without even a drop of oil for moisture. Perhaps you'd like a little cabbage, Herr Mizel?' Kisch pointed to the dish before him with his fork, fes-tooned with a straggling strand of grey-white cabbage. 'And you, Herr Ritter? Don't you like cabbage? Cabbage is good for the lungs, I tell you.'

'No, thank you.'

'Perhaps you, Herr Adler?'

'No!'

'That's not good, Herr Adler,' Kisch added amid some noisy lip-smacking. 'Believe me, last week you lost three hundred grams in weight, and that isn't good. Trust me, I have experience: there's nothing better for the lungs than cabbage, and lots of it. Eating is the key to everything! Simple!'

'But Herr Kisch'— Adler smiled —'I haven't lost weight at all. On the contrary, last week I gained half a kilo.'

'That's what I'm saying, sir, it isn't enough! Half a kilo is very little for those with tubercular issues. You should be gaining a kilo every week, at the very least one kilo. That is the minimum, I tell you. Look, for example, at Herr Ritter.' Kisch pointed with his fork to the latter, who sat there full of potatoes, his face red and sweaty. 'He's your friend, sir, isn't he? Your room-mate, I believe. Take a look, without prejudice. This is a patient after my own heart. He can be relied on to do the job properly! The lung is not to be underestimated, I'm telling you — it demands a great deal of attention, gentlemen. And the essential element: eating, gorging yourself! Fattening up the damaged areas! Believe me.'

'But you yourself have gained nothing this last week, have you?' Seberg the engineer interrupted him with derision.

'I? For that there is a reason, sir; everything has a reason. I was suffering from a cold; I was coughing. My stomach was not in working order, and yet I gained five hundred grams all the same. Gained, I tell you! But it was very little, next to nothing, sir!'

'And am I not right, Herr Levy, eh?' Kisch continued after a short pause for chewing. 'With you too, sir, I feel some satisfaction; with you and with Herr Ritter. Not so the engineer — sauce and soup? Where is the substance, I ask! Will gravy heal the lung? Good for fertility but no good for the lung! Potatoes, cabbage, cabbage especially, gentlemen,' Herr Kisch insisted, pointing to the dish before him.

Little Mizel had already turned bright red with repressed contempt — that Czech bastard! Now Kisch could restrain himself no longer. He also curled his fleshy lips into a sneer and said: 'Herr Mizel here, now this is someone I love … a clever lad! He's from Prague too — hurrah! A charming youth indeed.'

Most had already finished the main course and were waiting for their dessert. Frau Schnabel, a tall, lean, and nosy woman of about forty, was already wiping her red face with a big handkerchief and panting like a steam engine. As well as two dishes of soup, she had already crammed into herself two portions of meat, bread, and glasses of water — and several mounds of potatoes. No one knew where these stacks of food disappeared to. She always stayed as thin as she was. The girls in her vicinity nudged one another and laughed.

Adler's eyes briefly made contact with those of Rachel Portugal, who sat as if she had been removed thousands of miles from here.

How beautiful she is, this girl! Adler thought. *For her alone it's worth staying in the sanatorium!*

Ilsa Dohan, who until now had been stacking up the potatoes with prodigious dedication, finally took her eyes from the dish, and was sitting erect. Her permanently pale face was flushed now from the chin to the black hair that flopped over her forehead, and her blue eyes, big and dreamy, wandered this way and that.

'Her anger has subsided,' said Seberg the engineer.

Adler puffed out his jaws at her, hinting that she would grow fat this way, and she laughed and flashed her pretty little teeth at him.

It was good for Adler to look into the marvellous eyes of Ilsa Dohan; he had never seen eyes like those before.

Fischer the violinist, sitting next to the engineer, took a notebook and a pencil from his pocket, and gestured to Ilsa that he was going to draw her portrait. Fischer's tanned, gloomy face resembled that of a bony Croatian, and his brown eyes, shrewd and incisive, were like a pair of beetles.

Ilsa Dohan pretended to take it seriously, and she sat motionless. Fischer took notes, looking at the girl from time to time and then sketching obscene images, while chortling with his whole face.

Then from a distance he showed her the picture, covering part of it with his hand so that its true nature could not be ascertained, and asked her with a gesture if she liked the artwork. The boys around him were doubled up with laughter.

On the table in front of her, Lyuba Goldis placed a little chocolate-coloured rubber doll, whose head was bigger than the rest of its body, the big whites of its eyes turning right and left. From time to time Lyuba turned to Richard Berlin, lifting the doll to show him and stretching out a tongue like a red-hot dagger.

Greta Finger's eyes searched for Adler's, and he pretended not to notice.

And Marishka Cohen, with her black, cropped, curly hair, turned her lorgnette, raising it now and again with a steady, practised movement to her short-sighted eyes, assessing those around the table. On her knowing mouth, the ghost of a faint smile hovered all the time, as if saying: *We already know all this … it's not interesting anymore …*

Just as she did every day at lunchtime, the vice-president appeared in the doorway of the kitchen: Frau-Doktor Wolf in her black hat and white gown over her black dress, and her friendly old face radiant with goodwill, spreading serenity and confidence in the invalids' hearts.

After dessert the invalids rose, satisfied and in a jovial mood.

'I'm short of breath,' complained Ritter, whose asthma seemed to have been exacerbated by the plentiful food to the point of pressure on the lung. 'There's no air!'

The women went into the gloomy corridor and waited for the lift, which intermittently returned from above, collected a handful of them, and took them up. The youths surrounded them, whispering to them, making plans to pair up for the four p.m. walk.

'The superintendent, the superintendent!' The whispered warning was thrown into the fray. The boys dispersed at once. The first-floor occupants escaped behind the glass door and went up in groups to their rooms.

Preparations were underway for the afternoon nap. Doors slammed; felt slippers shuffled over the smooth linoleum in the long corridor.

Adler had lit himself a furtive cigarette and hidden it in a partially open drawer of the table. He took a surreptitious drag from it now and then as he stripped off his clothes.

'Don't worry,' said Ritter, entering the room. 'No one's coming now.'

Adler waved the towel this way and that like some strange kind of spell, and wafted towards the door, open to the balcony, the blue smoke that stagnated in the air in a mass of lines, whirls, and tendrils.

While stripping off his clothes, Ritter exerted the glands of his large nose and struggled, through his chronic congestion, to catch a whiff of the cigarette smoke.

'No,' he assured Adler, 'nothing to smell now!'

'The filter is a little hot, Ritter, old pal, don't you think?' shouted Karl Levy from the balcony, while flicking a piece of orange peel at the other's bare back.

'Wait, yellow liar' — Ritter laughed — 'I'm on to you!'

Gibes, jokes, and bits of orange peel flew back and forth along the balcony. Upstairs, the women cackled derisively. Some of them poked heads swathed in colourful towels over the balustrade and peeped down. Rolly Reicher lowered a rope, and the boys tied it to Ornik's pillow. When he was about to lay his head on it, the pillow suddenly rose from the bench and began its ascent, to the laughter of all.

'Rolly again!' Ornik whispered with a good-natured smile, as he watched the pillow rising. His heavy head remained idly suspended for a moment.

'What is this? What is to become of your rest-time, gentlemen?' Sister Lisl suddenly shouted in her damaged voice with its Tyrolean accent.

The boys leaped to their own benches and lay down.

Porges, Karl Levy's room-mate, sat on the chair beside his bench, his long, fleshy back turned towards the sun. On a wooden frame before him stood a mirror, and another one, small and round, which he held by its long silver handle, was positioned in his gaping mouth, and in this way he diverted the sun's rays towards his tubercular throat.

'Will you be finishing soon, Porges? Time to sleep!' Levy urged him.

Ritter laid his body down, naked except for a pair of short underpants, and surrendered it to the sunlight. He intoned with restrained delight: 'Ah, how very pleasant — a little sunshine like this, you won't find anywhere else!'

Very gradually, the designated 'total relaxation' of the afternoon took over the sanatorium. A heavy orange sun was suspended over the entire valley. Over the top of the dense stillness, the deep, blue skies were shimmering, and the snow was turning blue on the mountain crags, radiating a bright, dazzling light. The tram passed, clattering and scraping, and moved on to Lana. Far away, behind the houses shrouded by the greening trees, the train's siren sounded on the dam: a sharp blast, muffled and distorted at the end. The clatter of the wheels rang out. It was the train that crossed the border, that would traverse the valleys stretching hundreds of leagues between the Alpine ridges of Carinthia and Styria, that would propel itself through the dark and winding crevices, and early the next morning would arrive in awakening Vienna.

Most of the patients were already asleep. Ritter snored like a sawmill.

'A swarm of buzzing insects,' muttered Karl Levy in a nasal, sleepy voice, as he turned on his side.

The sun wallowed on Adler's naked body, scorching his chest like a blazing bandage. Gentle exhalations hovered from time to time over his inflamed chest, spreading and escaping behind the shoulders to his sweat-soaked back. His brain felt heavy, molten, in his skull, and when Adler moved his head, it seemed he could physically hear his brain bubbling from inside, as if liquefied. Despite his fatigue, it was impossible for him to sleep.

Vienna — the thought was trapped in his mind — there, it was winter now, cold, snowing. But there, there was no infection of the lung. There were no lungs in Vienna. Sometimes, while scanning the paper, he saw a report about the tuberculosis that had been rife in recent years, but it seemed so remote, so extreme — no one believed it; no one took notice of it. A man wrapped himself in a cloak and was no longer afraid of the cold. Or he went and sat in a warm café, on an upholstered sofa, just sat. Through the big window, harassed passers-by would be visible, along with hurrying automobiles, big wagons festooned on all sides with empty liquor kegs, heavy black wagons carrying coal, men pulling handcarts, bicycle riders, a gigantic horse that had slipped and fallen on the icy pavement and was holding up the traffic, and so forth. But lungs — there were none.

'What's the time, Herr Adler?' asked Ritter sleepily.

From below, from the bottom balcony, a crash was suddenly heard, like the sound of breaking glass. Following close behind it, the monotonous voice of Herr Kisch, as if he were reading from a book: 'Gentlemen, a little quiet would do no harm.'

Meanwhile the sun was already receding, and had sunk below the summit of the hill, like a cockerel sitting on a beam to roost between suns. The cold was setting in.

'Time to get up, gentlemen!' Ritter stood up to wipe his sweaty face with a handkerchief. There were furrows and livid, rose-pink weals on his broad back, etched by the creases in the mattress. He went to the washbasin and rinsed his sunburned body.

'Ah,' he panted, 'a wash in cold water is so nice after the sun! The body is toughened and capable of enduring the chill.'

Karl Levy came in from the balcony. His full face, flushed with freckles strewn under his watery eyes, smiled with satisfaction.

'You're not letting me sleep, my friend,' Levy complained, 'snoring like a sawmill!'

'Who's snoring?'

'You, Ritter, you and your nose in person!'

'Impossible — I've hardly slept at all. Five minutes perhaps ...'

'But you were definitely snoring — all through the "total relaxation"!' Karl Levy lowered his voice a little and turned his mind to what he came in for. 'At last I'm going to get her, you'll see!'

'Get who?'

'Oh, Schneider, of course! I'm holding things up on purpose … first let her squirm for a bit.'

'Take care you're not the one who ends up squirming,' said Ritter, rubbing his back with a rough towel. 'She's crafty, that Schneider.'

'You think that's going to happen to me? No, my friend — if so, you don't know me yet! It's about ambition on my part, just ambition and nothing more. She thinks I'm harmless, reckons I've fallen in love with her … it doesn't bother me at all!'

Karl Levy took a few paces across the room, and came back and stood before Ritter as he dressed. 'You know, she told me she has a boyfriend in Vienna, but nothing's happened between them yet: she didn't want it …'

'It's possible.'

'She's probably all steamed up, red-hot for it. I reckon she's still a virgin.'

'And how far have you got?' Ritter asked, like a man of the world.

'Well, the plans have been laid; I've set up the battle-field' — Levy smiled a devious smile — 'and I'm delaying the main event on purpose. Besides, I haven't got a venue yet. She isn't going to lie down under the open sky, and I don't care for things that are too rushed and hasty.'

'Book yourself a room in some hotel,' Ritter advised.

'I'll be doing that too. I've already contacted the Sentinel Hotel.' In Levy's watery eyes, two pale, lustful flames were flashing.

After a moment Levy started again. 'Doctor Macleese has

his eye on her; he visits their room regularly. Once, she told me, he wanted to kiss her, when Trudi was in the room …'

'The dirty monkey!'

'This morning, you know, he wanted to join us on the walk. I winked at her, at Schneider, and she told him we were going to visit friends who'd come from Vienna. He tries it on with all of them,' Levy continued, 'he gives them injections in the thigh, the girls … Not long ago Greta Finger ran out of the surgery with tears in her eyes. No one knows what happened there. He even tried to kiss Trudi …'

'How do you know?' Ritter jumped as if bitten.

'Schneider told me.'

'Liar! She's lying!' cried Ritter, all fired up. His blue elastic braces, which he had been busy fastening to the front buttons of his trousers, flew out of his hand. 'She's out to slander Trudi. I'll ask her — Trudi wouldn't lie …

'That Galician insect!' Ritter fumed and searched on the table for his round horn-rimmed glasses, as if without them he couldn't see well enough to be angry. 'He'll find out what kind of a man I am! Not for nothing was I at war, four years! Four years in the trenches! I'll burn him out of the Albano: he'll be out of here tomorrow! To be molesting sick, defenceless girls …

'But she's lying, that Schneider!' Ritter consoled himself for a moment. 'Every word she says is a lie.'

The beating of the gong was heard from the corridor. Karl Levy said as he went out, 'Anyway, there's no point in getting worked up about it. Maybe the whole thing's make-believe.'

Ritter dressed carefully, silently, full of murderous revenge.

Towards the evening Irma Ornik stood before the basin and washed his mouth out, which was his habit before and after a meal. He would wash it three times: first with plain water, then with manganese water, and finally with Odol water. Then he put the cup down and turned on the tap to wash away the red-purple traces of manganese, which remained scattered over the white enamel. A sharp coolness, permeated with the smell of Odol, lingered for a little while longer in his mouth. It was a pleasurable sensation.

The invalids had gone out for a stroll and the clinic was engulfed in total silence. From outside, the greying evening skies were visible. Ornik was now feeling, to his surprise, no particular discomfort, something which had not been his lot in days and months. But a kind of heavy dullness, the sort that is felt during a summer heatwave before the rain comes, was diffused throughout his large body. Ornik turned on the electric light, retrieved from his bedside-table drawer the letter-writing paper and the Waterman pen that he had bought himself a few weeks ago and allowed no one else to touch, for reasons of hygiene, and sat down to finish his letter to Doctor Kalbol, which he had begun writing in the morning. In small, pinched script he wrote:

… The air is good here, perhaps better than in Alland, as I had the privilege of mentioning in my previous letter. But

[35]

its effect on my health isn't perceptible. My condition has not improved: the phlegm is as copious as ever and not uncontaminated by blood, my temperature is usually high, and there are stabbing pains and other persistent twinges, as you will appreciate, Herr Doktor, on the basis of a temperature chart such as this. It even seems to me I'm coughing a little more here. In general I cough between ten and fifteen times on a fine day, more when it's rainy or cloudy. Abrupt and hollow coughs, usually without phlegm. Do you think, esteemed Herr Doktor, that there is a possibility that in spite of this my condition may become chronic? Although I have not reached that point yet, there is always the danger of a haemorrhage!

The doctor in charge of this institution is not at all reliable. Doctor Volk, the senior physician, understands a little, perhaps, but he's virtually invisible. He visits the sanatorium on rare occasions, and very briefly, and there's never enough time to talk to him properly.

Needless to say, I treat myself with the utmost caution, paying close attention to my condition, and I don't deviate by so much as a hair's breadth from the routine that I have established for myself. A few days ago I allowed myself to go out walking for twenty minutes, no more. I was walking very slowly, of course — and yet I became very tired. I was covered in sweat, and my temperature also increased by five-tenths of a degree. Since then I have been more careful.

The medications that you prescribed for me, Herr Doktor, at our last meeting, I am consuming as before — secretly, of course. Should I buy another bottle when this one is used up?

I should add that today, as it happens, I am feeling no pain, and last night I slept better — hopefully this trend will continue.

The patients were required to take their temperatures and count their pulse rates four times a day. But Ornik was measuring his every two hours; and as for his temperature chart, he was preparing two simultaneously, one of them for Doctor Kalbol, a precise journal in which he meticulously recorded — besides his temperature, pulse rate, and bowel movements, all of which was information required of the other patients — everything that, in his opinion, might have a bearing on the status of his indisposition: intermittent pain, insomnia, night sweats, nocturnal pollutions, nosebleeds, quantities of phlegm expectorated, variations in body weight, and the treatments and medications currently on offer.

Ornik tucked his letter away in a big envelope, enclosed his temperature chart for the past two weeks, and walked slowly downstairs to hand it to Herman the janitor, for posting. When he had returned to his room and hidden his writing implements, he sat for a while on the chair, and gave his attention to what was happening inside him, listening to every limb and every organ individually. No — there really was no perceptible sensation in him! Ornik stood up, put on his red turban, spat into the portable spittoon that he carried in his pocket, wrapped himself in his cloak, and was about to go out to the balcony and lie down — and suddenly he felt a twitch in his right cheek. Not an explicit pain, but a rather unpleasant burning sensation. He went to the basin and washed his mouth out again with manganese water, but the sensation did not subside.

Outside, it was already dark. Cold, sharp air streamed in through the slightly open door. Ah — Ornik understood the reason for his discomfort: he had forgotten to close the door, and his teeth must have got cold while he was writing. Such lack of caution! As long as it didn't develop into another gum infection! A moment ago he had written to Doctor Kalbol, informing him that he was feeling no pain that day; hopefully the letter was still in Herman's hand.

Ornik did not hesitate and went down again to the janitor's cubby-hole, but the letter was no longer there. Ornik went back to his room. He suddenly felt very tired and utterly deserted.

Meanwhile it was already five, and the hasty steps of the invalids, returning from their walk, sounded in the corridor. Seberg the engineer came in carrying his coat and hat, which he had already removed on the stairs, and said in jest, 'It seems you're starting to neglect things, Ornik!'

'Why?' the other asked in a whisper.

'You haven't come out yet for your evening nap.'

'I have toothache. I'll lie down on my bed.'

'No, no,' the engineer protested, as if foreseeing some danger for him. 'Better to go out on the balcony! Nothing's going to happen to you!'

Ornik stripped off his clothes slowly and lay down on his bed.

After the evening meal Adler went in to visit Ornik, who had been lying in bed for the past few days. A pungent blend of iodine, codeine, cognac, Odol, and soap hung in the air. Ornik's jaws were swaddled in a big white towel, which swallowed up most of his round face. A white and orange blanket was pulled down to his stomach, and through his open bed-shirt his white, hairy chest peeped out.

Seberg the engineer, who was sitting at the table and busily copying a female nude from an illustrated magazine, got up and offered Adler his chair.

'How are you, Ornik?'

'Bad!' Ornik whispered, as if so critically ill that his voice were affected too. 'My teeth! And the whole left side of my head. The cheek is all swollen — a real gum infection. Besides that I've got a high temperature, and stabbing pains in my lungs.'

'You're just malingering, Ornik!' Seberg interjected. 'Unwrap your teeth and get out of bed.'

On the night-table at the head of the bed stood two little bottles containing coloured pills, and arranged beside them were three thermometers and the blue spittoon, almost full to the brim. On the chair beside the bed, piled up on top of one another, were several books in old bindings, and Ornik's clothes hanging on the back.

'What are you reading here, Ornik?' asked Adler, nodding towards the books.

'Reading?' Ornik was bemused, as if suspected of a crime. 'No, I'm not reading anything. The books have just been left there. It's been a year and a half since I read anything.'

'Why is that?' Adler asked, interested.

'I'm not entitled ...'

'Not entitled to what?' Adler wondered if he had heard correctly.

'No, I'm not entitled,' Ornik repeated with solemnity. 'I mustn't divert my attention from my lungs. My parents are going without bread so they can send me everything I need, and it's been a year and a half. Have you any idea of just how long that is? *A whole year and a half!* And I'm going to amuse myself reading books and neglect my lungs?'

'But dwelling obsessively on a disease doesn't help, Ornik. On the contrary, it leads to emotional stress and high blood pressure.'

'The sick man has no right' — Ornik wasn't budging — 'to be a burden on others; he doesn't even have the right to breathe the air! Especially the lung patient. He endangers the healthy with every breath; he fills the air with malignant particles. Do you know, Herr Adler,' Ornik whispered as if sharing a secret, and smiled a crazy smile, 'in my opinion they should be destroyed — give them drugs and wipe them out once and for all!'

'Who?'

'The patients of course! The lung patients ...'

'Correct!' the engineer said, to test him. 'We have a sacred duty to destroy Ornik. Give him drugs, only drugs!'

'You're wrong, Ornik, for as long as a man is breathing, he's entitled to the air. More than that, he's committed to it! He shouldn't give up on even a sixtieth of a second of his life.'

'It doesn't apply to anyone else,' the engineer persisted, his eyes laughing, 'but Ornik needs to be removed from the world! A sacred duty, I say. A man who lies in bed and constantly invents new maladies for himself and disturbs the peace of his neighbours — let's poison him and be done with it!'

Ornik smiled into his towel. His thick beetling brows, which in one black line crossed the width of his forehead, overshadowed his dark eyes, making it impossible now to peer into their depths.

'Last night,' the engineer went on, 'I woke up suddenly to a terrible racket. I turn on the light and Ornik is sitting up in his bed, waving his fists and fighting — with whom do you suppose, Herr Adler? You'll never guess, I promise you! He's sitting there and fighting *the wall* … raining blows on it according to all the rules of boxing. "Bochi," he snorted like a maniac, "I'll smash your skull, bastard! I'll cut off your leg and use it to bolt the door, ha-ha-ha!" If he hadn't woken up he would have destroyed that wall. Now, you tell me, should a man like that be allowed to go on living?'

'Not true.' Ornik laughed awkwardly. 'The engineer has made it all up. I only knocked against the wall with my elbow.'

'Get out of bed, Ornik!' the engineer repeated, objecting for some reason to Ornik's supine posture. 'Get up and get dressed and stop treating yourself for imaginary diseases. There's a social event this evening: go down and spend some time with the girls!'

'I don't need girls,' said Ornik, who suddenly felt a pain in his gums as if a long nail was rammed in there. 'No need and no right …'

'All the same,' said Adler as he rose from the chair, 'you have to be strong, Ornik! Read something and distract your mind for a while. You'll see, after one week you'll feel so much better.'

Adler went out to the now-empty corridor and walked along it on the slippery dull-red linoleum, which glinted with a yellowish sheen under the electric light. Something heavy, which he didn't recognise, was turning over inside him. He stood for a while by the window at the end of the corridor, and looked out at the dense darkness of the night, then resumed his perambulation.

Annie, the flunkey of the women's floor, came down from above with a big white jug of milk, walking with a clumsy peasant's gait and swaying from side to side. Annie's hair was curly and as black as pitch, and her dark, forever-laughing eyes shone with southern, insistent fire. *These are the kind of women you dream about in your fevers,* thought Adler, *women of the night and of blazing heat ...*

Annie moved towards Adler with a smile. For some time she had felt that he was eyeing her; he knew when she would be passing by and waited for her.

Adler glanced around and then followed her, catching her by her fleshy arm and, in the process, pressing the back of his hand on her abundant breast. 'My brunette beauty, why do we never see you in our parts, on the first floor?'

Annie stood on the stairs and laughed, her mouth shining with little white teeth like those of a mouse, and on her round, swarthy cheeks two dimples appeared, quite irresistible.

'I have no time,' Annie apologised. 'Too much work.'

'Come into Betty's room for a moment, please,' Adler both demanded and pleaded. 'They're all downstairs now in the social room.'

'Not now — I have to fetch the milk.'

'Then when can you? When?'

'Another time. Maybe tomorrow. I was in Betty's room at lunchtime — where were you?'

'I didn't know, Annie, I didn't know.'

'Right. Betty will tell you when I'm coming … and now I must hurry.' Annie extricated herself from his hand and escaped to the kitchen.

Adler stayed there for some time, stunned. He felt exhaustion in his knees, and his head was blazing. He was like a man who had run with the last vestiges of his strength for the train, only for it to set off the moment he reached it.

Social evenings, or 'conjugal parties', as the jokers called them, took place twice a week. The youths would gather in the hall, which was adjacent to the dining room and set aside for this purpose, and while away in one another's company one hour of their existence in the sanatorium, from eight to nine p.m.

When Adler came in, there were already some twenty people in the room. Some stood by the open bookcase and flicked through the books with their tattered binding and yellowing pages: mostly works of classical litera-ture, and illustrated magazines dating back fifty years, which had already absorbed the sweat of thousands of sickly hands and tubercular bacteria by the million. Some sat at one of the tables, boys and girls, chattering and laughing. One group gathered around the big grand piano, which stood in the corner close to the door, leafing through the stacks of sheet music, and some nameless person struck the keys with an untrained hand and produced primitive, truncated chords from some operetta or song. It was hot, the air heavy and throbbing.

Kisch came in.

'Ah, Herr Kisch!'

'Good evening, Herr Kisch!'

'Gentlemen,' said Kisch, his eyes contracting in the hint of a smile, 'gentlemen, a little less noise would do no harm.'

'Over here, Herr Kisch!'

'Come and join us!'

'Here's a chair for you!'

Kisch sat down slowly on the chair that had been vacated for him beside the piano. In a flash the gang seized him and lifted him and the chair high up in the air.

Kisch waved his arms above their heads, his whole unshaven face flushing, and yelled, raising his voice by only one tone above the normal register. 'Gentlemen, I say … this is not the conduct of intelligent people … I … the chair could break!'

The gang roared with laughter. 'No, no, don't worry, Herr Kisch, the chair won't break!'

'Gentlemen' — Kisch threatened them from above — 'gentlemen, I can take a joke … But to everything there has to be a limit, a boundary, I tell you! When the boundary is crossed — I am a hard man.'

Kisch was put down again and stood there, red and fuming.

'We've made you our president, Herr Kisch! From this day on, you are our president!'

'A good joke in its time,' Kisch raged, 'and in the right degree! Everything in proportion! But when you cross the line, I tell you: beware of Herr Kisch! Even a slapping from me isn't out of the question, not where I'm concerned … I'm warning you; it won't end well! Don't ever cross the line! And you, Herr Mizel' — Kisch turned to the youngster who was standing beside him and laughing — 'you're just a lad, I'm telling you, a lad! From Prague!'

'Why are you getting so worked up, Herr Kisch?' asked Lyuba Goldis, who until now had sat whispering to Richard Berlin in a corner, both of them with flushed faces and sparkling eyes.

'Who's getting worked up? I'm not worked up at all.' Kisch smiled his most lascivious smile at her. 'I only said it's necessary to observe the appropriate measure. The principle: everything in proportion. Is it not so, Fräulein Goldis?'

'Of course, of course, Herr Kisch is right! That is precisely the point.' Lyuba Goldis laughed.

'Herr Kisch is right!'

'Long live the president!' The gang got behind Lyuba Goldis.

'Gentlemen, a little less noise would do no harm,' protested young Mizel, narrowing his cunning eyes.

'Very true,' Kisch agreed with the hint of a smile. 'I love Herr Mizel! A very astute young man.'

Meanwhile the hall was filling up. The heat was intense, as was the noise, and there was no air to breathe. Adler wandered round alone, pausing for a moment beside one group or another, his mood thoroughly sour.

'Come and sit with us for while, Adler old boy!' The invitation came from Greta Finger, sitting with Seberg the engineer.

Adler joined them and sat morosely with his elbows propped on the table. 'What secrets are you going to share, Greta my treasure?' he teased her.

'You tell us, Adler; you're cleverer than we are ...'

'It seems to me you're a little bit in love, Greta dear, your eyes radiate love ...'

'Not just a little bit, not a little bit at all. I'm out of my mind with love.' Greta Finger laughed, exposing big teeth, rather too big for a woman.

'And who is the one you love?'

'Well, work it out for yourself, old boy, you have a keen eye after all.'

'I bet it's the engineer.' Adler nodded in his direction.

'What am I worth that I should hope?' The engineer laughed.

'You haven't worked it out yet?'

'Who is it, then?'

'Why, it's you, my dear ... only you, alone!' Greta laughed. 'And from the first moment I laid eyes on you!'

'Really? I had no idea ...' Adler affected an air of dignity.

The engineer smiled. His grey-green eyes were damp and his forehead was sweating.

'And if I don't return your love, Greta my darling,

I expect you to kill yourself — is that right?'

'Of course, of course, I shall hang myself at once ... I shall hang myself on the engineer, if he'll let me, or on dear old Ornik, or on Herman ...'

'Aha! On Herman! Definitely, on Herman alone,' Adler jested.

Lyuba Goldis was out of control, her face ablaze and her wavy hair dishevelled, laughing and speaking coarse, broken German, clutching with her thin and slightly overlong hands at this one and that, urging them to play Blind Cow. At once they grabbed Herr Kisch, tied a handkerchief over his eyes, and stood in a wide circle around him, and he moved around with mouth agape, flailing the air with his outstretched hands, while the assembled company harassed him from front and back, escaping his clutches with laughter and squeals. Kisch grabbed hold of one girl and fumbled at her, groping her body and her face, and concluding, 'Lyuba Goldis!'

'No!' yelled the chorus, and the game carried on.

Then Fischer the violinist came in, bringing his violin with him. He took the instrument from its grey linen case, put it to his shoulder, gripped it with his fleshy, sun-burned chin, and started playing his trademark Fibich poem, which he played whenever the opportunity arose. Fischer's perceptive, moody eyes wandered this way and that, looking with suppressed anger at anyone who dared to make a sound.

Adler was suddenly filled with intense fury at this boy, for forcing him to listen to his scratching. He went to the door with the intention of going out, and then he saw

Rachel Portugal, who had just come in. Adler greeted her and remained standing close to her, near the door.

Rachel Portugal was in a sour mood for some reason. In her black eyes was an expression of gloom, and the corners of her mouth receded from time to time. She looked at Adler, and it seemed she didn't see him at all, only something behind him.

'Are you sad, Fräulein?' said Adler with concern. 'Has something happened?'

'No,' the girl replied briefly, cutting him off.

Suddenly Adler felt grieved, sorely grieved. All at once the full weight of the predicament was obvious to him, his predicament and the predicament of all these young people, standing and sitting here with flushed faces and inflamed eyes. Adler felt a choking in his throat. He wanted so much now to laugh, laugh out loud, wrap himself up in laughter and pain. Adler's eyes, blue and pure like a baby's, widened and filled with tears for a brief moment, but one moment only. And Rachel Portugal took in, with a random glance, that hasty expression in his eyes, and felt that this Adler was very close to her in a certain sense, close to her on the inside, like the closeness that a shared disaster created between strangers.

Rachel Portugal wanted to give Adler some special, encouraging word.

'Are you staying until the end, Herr Adler?' she asked in a caressing voice.

'What?' Adler woke up. 'Oh, yes ... I mean, no. I'm not staying! I shall be leaving in another four weeks. It's hard here, in such a crowded place ... and you, Fräulein?'

'I suppose I'll stay. Even though it's hard for me too. But every person wants to regain his health.'

In the doorway Herman the janitor appeared, a tough and jaundiced Tyrolean, coming to remind them that the hour was up.

Soon the common room was empty, and all the invalids returned to their beds.

If there were, in the sanatorium, things capable of astonishing and distracting during the day, the night was utterly uninhibited, and all kinds of depressing thoughts could tyrannise the patients without fear of interference.

The patients would spend all day lying down, occasionally going out for walks, dozing in the afternoons; and while they were usually exhausted as a result of the sickness itself, and because of the warm evenings — in addition to this, they were trapped almost permanently in a state of disquiet, of morbid wakefulness, and it was hard for them to fall asleep at nine-thirty, the prescribed bedtime in the sanatorium.

The night sky arched over the valley like an inverted cauldron, with innumerable specks of light within. The hills around were piled up like dim and exceedingly heavy building blocks. Here and there gleamed the little golden light of some remote house. Rising up and filtering through to this place from an unidentified distant source was an exuberant, sentimental drinking-song, hoarse and broken lyrics set to a lilting Italian melody, which would pause for a moment and start up again. And a very thin, congealed chill would unwittingly penetrate the overheated lung, slashing with imperceptible cuts like those of a sharp razor.

Oh, great was the night of that mountain wilderness, great and free and beautiful and sad in no small measure. Here, unlike in the town, one could meet it face to face — there was nowhere to take refuge. And its message would be something like: *Let's see who prevails over whom ... Think your thoughts through to the end, and even a little beyond that; think!*

In the half-light of his room, Ornik's head, swathed in a towel and resembling a bundle of cotton wool, merged with the whiteness of the pillow underneath it. Overlaying it all was the heavy smell of iodine, which he had recently smeared on his stinging gums. His body was ablaze and the fingers of his right hand, they only, were wet with sweat. Ornik took out his right hand and laid it on the blankets. An obstinate pain throbbed in his gums, from lower to upper, throbbed regularly and rhythmically, like a drip from a tap that has not been properly shut.

Lying down was hard for Ornik. *Now, now of all times —* a strange idea occurred to him — *it would be good to run away ...* Ornik didn't know where he would run to, didn't even know for certain whom or what he was running from; but a compulsive desire lit up in him, to run in the darkness of the night, run like a lunatic until all his strength was exhausted. A blazing fire flared up in Ornik: he was boiling like a steam locomotive, and it took him all his strength to restrain himself, to stop himself leaping out of his bed.

Rising before his eyes was a series of episodes from recent years, paraded in order, abstract, vague, precise. Here there were days, weeks, months, one alongside the other;

of unremitting confinement to sanatoriums, where he was always supine save for a few hours of feeble crawling: long, hard death-throes. Ornik's mind was becoming confused. *And the end of it?* the question reverberated in him. Ornik suddenly felt the reality of the heavy burden of his gigantic body, as if he were carrying it in one hand. And thus Ornik was thinking at that hour of darkest night:

Here he is, the whole length of the bed and half its width, a heavy and stricken load — Ornik! One metre and eighty-four centimetres of Ornik! A complex amalgam of Budapest and Vienna, of the elite academy and business school, of disease and sanatorium. And behold: facing him is a world great and full, with the splendour of days and nights, the happiness and the tribulations of creativity — and all this is apparently beautiful, to a breathtaking degree, but in Ornik's eyes the whole thing is wondrous and closed ... and he most certainly does not grasp the significance of the links in the chain, strung together, each with its neighbour, until the end of things and their beginning. He, Ornik, after all, is one of these links, perhaps an important one, in the opinion of Sebag Adler, and every breath of air that he inhales has been ready and waiting for him since the six days of creation, it's for him, and no one has the right to take it from him. How is it possible then, that in spite of all this he sees himself as an outsider, outside the whole world and tarnishing it? Will the world and Ornik just go on harassing each other?

It was already late when Ornik fell asleep while in the throes of these demented thoughts, absurd fragments of which continued to bother him persistently in his fitful sleep.

A few days later, one morning, Irma Ornik hauled his large body, slowly and cautiously, some distance away from the sanatorium. His big hands were hanging at his sides, somewhat detached from the stooped body, completely inactive and superfluous, and on his face, shaded by the fringes of his crumpled black hat, that characteristic expression of unshakeable calm was engraved, unshakeable and slightly foolish. A day of intense sunshine once more swamped the Albano Valley, the houses and the smart hotels immersed in vivid green, and the majestic mountains all around.

On the bridge Greta Finger caught up with him. 'Should I believe my eyes, Ornik? Are you truly and honestly going for a walk, without being afraid of anything?'

'Yes, I decided to stroll for half an hour.' Ornik smiled bashfully. Greta broke her stride and walked for a while beside him. Then she asked if he wanted to accompany her to the market; there was something she needed to buy.

'Of course … nothing would give me greater pleasure, madame,' Ornik stammered awkwardly, 'but —'

'What's the "but" for?' Greta interrupted him with a confident laugh, her grey-green eyes fixed sidelong on his immobile face. 'Perhaps you have an engagement now with a young lady …'

'No, absolutely not!' Ornik assured her innocently. 'But … it's difficult walking with me; I mustn't hurry …'

'I'll walk very slowly. I'll crawl like a crab — like this!' Greta demonstrated for his benefit, hopping and tripping along with minuscule steps.

Ornik walked on, against his will, alongside the girl, who barely reached his shoulder, and was silent. He felt a kind of pressure, as if he were being squeezed by the malign forces of this over-populated world. Why had this girl latched on to him? Yet in spite of this, he found it agreeable in some obscure corner inside him.

Ornik was feeling the heat, and his short coat was becoming heavy. He was quite unaware that he was already walking like any other person, and although there was nothing athletic about his gait, it was capable of covering distances.

'Don't you talk at all, Ornik?'

'What?' He was confused.

In silence they passed the end of the Rennweg, a broad thoroughfare where carriages harnessed to single horses stood all day on both sides and waited for the occasional passenger, and their drivers were gathered beside one of them, engaged in banal conversation and smoking cheap cigarettes. Then they turned to the narrow, dingy street of the market, where the old houses with the grey shutters were all built in the style of the Middle Ages, and decorated here and there on the outside with ornate inscriptions and pictures from the lives of the Christian saints. Along the two rows of shops were two warehouses, open to the street and covered by the overhanging upper storeys of the buildings, low and dingy spaces and always as chilly as cellars, serving as storage for all kinds of goods.

'You don't mind?' Greta entwined her arm with his as they entered the warehouse space to their right. Ornik suddenly felt a tingling in his limbs and a strange weariness, pleasant in a certain sense.

'Do you know Adler well?' Greta asked.

'Which Adler?'

'Well, that Adler, of course, our man!'

'I know him from here, from the sanatorium,' whispered Ornik, already short of breath, due to a combination of emotion and fast walking.

'A rather strange person, don't you think?'

'Strange? Possibly … yes, you could say that, strange.'

'And you, Ornik, are you not interested in girls at all?' asked Greta, partly in earnest and partly in jest.

'Me? I'm not well …' Ornik was thoroughly confused now.

Greta Finger went into a shop and pulled Ornik after her, although he would have preferred to wait outside. They opened a series of paper boxes full of silk stockings. Greta fingered a skin-coloured stocking, thrust her little hand into it and tested its stretch, studied it for a while, and asked Ornik, who was standing motionless beside her, tired and flustered, if he liked this colour.

'This colour … yes … I would say …' he stammered and didn't finish.

Then she bought another piece of fabric, three metres in length, paid for it, and handed the package to Ornik. Ornik took it in his right hand, transferred it to his left hand, as if it were a very heavy burden, and suddenly felt a stabbing pain in his lung. The image that flashed immediately in his mind was a dangerous haemorrhage — he saw himself laid out motionless on a bed, his mouth filling every few moments with a stream of warm, slightly salty blood, its odour vague and strange, almost imperceptible — and it seemed to him with absolute clarity that something was rising from his intestines to his throat. Ornik turned aside and took out the portable spittoon that he always carried in his pocket, and observed while spitting that this was nothing more than simple phlegm. Despite this he felt he was being tormented for no wrongdoing of his.

Outside, Greta bought a kilogram of apples from a stall, as well as a few oranges, and loaded everything on Ornik. On his face a look of great sorrow obtruded. He walked beside the girl, his body big and heavy and his hands full of packages, and it seemed to him that at any moment he would collapse under the heavy load. He was now absolutely certain that this walk would have serious consequences for him. In the broad, attractive Gitastrasse, Greta paused beside the display windows of several large stores; looked at shoes, dresses, and under-wear; and showed no inclination at all to return to the sanatorium. Ornik was in despair. Oh, he thought, his heart shrinking — if only he were there now, on his bench or in a bed.

Meanwhile the tower-clock was chiming — it was time to go back. Ornik walked with broad paces, something he hadn't done in a year and a half, and breathed heavily, his whole body bathed in sweat, red circles sprouting on his jaws.

'All the same,' said Greta suddenly, 'you should give a little more attention to the girls. A lot of them are interes-ted in you.'

In the corridor he finally handed the girl her packages. She said, 'Will you be going for a walk at four?'

'At four? I don't know. Maybe ... when I feel better.'

Ornik's excursion was a novelty to the other patients. In the boot room they teased him good-naturedly and asked if he'd remembered to take his temperature in the street.

'What's your condition, Herr Ornik?' Kisch smiled his oily smile. 'A little walk can do no harm, gentlemen.'

Ornik took off his shoes and dragged his heavy body up the stairs. His body somehow seemed to have gained even more weight, thanks to Greta Finger and her packages. His head was feverish and painful and full of incoherent thoughts. But beyond all the extensive weariness and his various typical sensations, he now felt in his right arm the smarting caused by the touch of Greta Finger's hand in the street near the market: he felt it with the utmost clarity, as if it were a severe wound, freshly inflicted.

What was the last thing she said? In his head, Ornik went over Greta's words as he lay down a few moments later on his bench under his grey booth. *A lot of them are interested in you ...* but what did he want with girls? The lung — that was what needed looking after; that was why he was here. And she, she herself, was she interested in him too? It would be good to know ... and how much sarcasm there was in her laughter, that one! No! At four, obviously, he wouldn't be going out! He only hoped the walk he had just taken would have no harmful effects. Why did he agree to accompany her? And his parents thought he was taking care of his lung properly. No, such a thing would not happen to him a second time!

That day Ornik missed two temperature checks.

In the spacious day room on the first floor, young men were standing or sitting at tables after their supper, and, as was usual any evening when a social event was not taking place, they played cards, dominoes, chess, mah-jong. Some of them merely looked on and offered advice, and the room flickered with conversations, laughter, coughing, exclamations. Faces were flushed, the temperature was high, eyes flashed in the yellow electric light.

Irma Ornik, who had decided to play fifteen minutes of chess that evening, sat stony-faced opposite his sparring partner Doctor Schamhaft, a physician and philosophical essayist from Prague, whose habit was to discuss the most mundane of subjects in long, convoluted articles, like those of German scientific writers, so verbose and oblique that their meaning can never be understood. With his bald head propped on the palm of his right hand, which was planted on the table, Doctor Schamhaft assessed his moves and Ornik's in a low voice, his broad mouth occasionally emitting a chuckle of satisfaction.

'If I were to move my queen, you see,' Doctor Schamhaft explained to his entourage of spectators, 'the pawn will be left undefended, and the knight will take him and open up a breach in this wall, agreed? Black is then doomed for sure, irrevocably. So what then? The only solution in this situation is as follows: to block his path by moving the castle — so very simple! And this ploy came to me quite by chance, by chance alone, since my intellect' — Doctor Schamhaft smiled with feigned humility — 'my intellect is feeble, incapable of devising such an ingenious move! In this game I have no great expertise; I am only a beginner, a beginner devoid of talent … and Ornik, who is now on the offensive, what do you think? In my opinion, he now has to move his queen one square, one square and no more, and thereby he will put me in jeopardy again …'

Adler paused beside them for a while and then went out to the corridor. The room opposite the day room, used for storing the milk jug and other dairy utensils for the first floor, and Sister Lisl's 'house medications', was now open, and Betty was sitting there rinsing out a stack of elongated white cups in a bowl of boiling water. Fleischmann, a tall and lanky youth who was a taxi driver from Teschen in Moravia, and young Windel were standing beside Betty, pinching her from time to time, sniggering and exchanging crude jokes with her.

Adler remained in the doorway, looking in.

'She isn't here!' Betty laughed, turning to Adler.

But from behind the door a faint rustling was heard. Adler peered in and found Annie hiding there, suppressing her giggles.

'What are you hiding for, my beauty, my gypsy?' Adler embraced her behind the door and massaged her full breasts thoroughly and intently.

'Let me go, Herr Adler.' Annie extricated herself from his arms with a sensuous movement, and her laughter etched a pair of dimples on her cheeks. 'Let me go, the superintendent might come in …'

Windel stood and watched, clearly enjoying the spectacle. 'There you are, Herr Adler is a man after my own heart!' he said. 'He goes straight to the heart of the matter and doesn't get sidetracked … all down to temperament!

That Viennese education — you spot it straight away …'

Adler whispered in Annie's ear: 'And when will we get to be alone, just the two of us alone together … when's your day off?'

'I'll let you know via Betty. We'll go out some time and have a little fun.' Annie added aloud, 'Well, now I have to make a move!'

Annie held out to Adler a big, bony hand, red from arduous work, winked at him with her laughing eyes, which were awash with lust and licentiousness, and receded with swaying steps.

'Taken a fancy to Annie, have you, Herr Adler?' Betty teased him with a laugh. 'But Herman has beaten you to it …'

'That doesn't matter, Frau Betty.' Adler pinched her as etiquette demanded. 'There's room for two.'

'Leave me alone, Herr Adler,' Betty rebuffed him, or so it seemed, but the somewhat lean face of this forty-year-old woman had come to life, and her black eyes, still young, were moist with desire. 'Why are you hanging around with old women?'

'These are the best years of your life right now, Frau Betty,' Adler flattered her with the ghost of a smile.

'You should have seen me a few years ago!' the house-maid boasted. 'I was quite a girl back then, hot stuff … how the boys used to fight over me, I'm telling you, till they drew blood! That's the way I used to be. "Meyerhoffer Betty" was famous, in Lana and all over the district!'

'You've had a lot of lovers, have you, Betty?' the lanky Fleischmann chipped in.

'Those were different times, completely different! Betty was Betty … days and nights it was all parties and amorous frolics. There wasn't one boy in the whole neighbourhood who wasn't smitten with Black Betty! All of them — and now you have to go,' Betty interrupted herself, 'the superintendent could walk in any moment.'

In the corridor Fleischmann said, 'That old witch: is she on fire or what! But she's still good, I reckon … what do you say?'

After a moment he whispered into Adler's ear, so Windel wouldn't hear, 'We'll work something out: the two of us and her and Annie … what the hell!'

Adler passed through his room and went out to the dark balcony, lit himself a cigarette, and inhaled surreptitiously. No sky now. In the impenetrable pall of darkness a few faint lights were floating some distance away. No houses, no hills — all erased. The air was mild and a little moist, meaning that the rains would be coming soon, Adler realised. At the end of the balcony Richard Berlin stood whispering to Lyuba Goldis, who was on the floor above. Voices and the sounds of laughter emerged from the day room. Betty moved from room to room, turning on lights, putting two cups of milk on two bedside cabinets, turning off lights, and leaving.

Meanwhile nine o'clock had arrived. Adler went into his room and started stripping off his clothes, taking occasional sips from the milk.

Ritter and Karl Levy burst into the room, in fits of mirth.

'How much did you win, you yellow cheat, you?' Levy laughed.

'Not much. About two kroner. And you?'

'I didn't lose either. Sister Lisl — the devil take her! If she'd let me finish, I'd have won this time too!'

They both went out again. After a moment Ritter came back looking scared. 'Quick, get into bed and turn out the light! Dr Volk is in the clinic.' He added in a whisper, while undressing, 'Have you heard, Herr Adler, Frau Potak is laid up again. Another haemorrhage! Tomorrow we'll have to send her flowers …'

Rain had been falling for several days without respite. The valley was awash with the pale-grey scraps of cloud that scudded close to the ground all day as if linked together. The houses and gigantic mountains were devoured by them. Sometimes, in the afternoon, the clouds took on a somewhat yellow hue, and a brown patch of the hillside was exposed. Then it seemed that in a little while the air would clear, but in no time at all the clouds returned and swaddled everything as before.

On the balconies the benches were laid lengthways against the wall, the foot of one nudging the head of another. Sharp gusts of rain descended diagonally, almost reaching the wall. The balcony floor was wet, and puddles were forming.

On days like this, most of the patients decided not to go out for walks, even though there was no specific prohibition against this. But lying down was excruciating too. Chilly moisture seeped relentlessly into the diseased lung and provoked fits of coughing. Wrapped up to their noses, which had turned red-blue, the patients lay with pale, angry faces, barely saying a word, but coughing and hawking incessantly. Now there was no doubting that the lung was sick, truly sick, and that there was no cure. It was as if the organ were excised and hung before the patient's eyes — a collapsed, perforated lung, full of green-gold phlegm.

An hour after the start of the evening nap Karl Levy returned from the town looking satisfied. He passed through Ritter's room and paused beside his bench, pushed partially inside through the open door.

Karl Levy's face was even redder than usual, and in his watery blue eyes was a flash like the gleam of glass.

'It's done!' said Levy with a smug expression.

'What's done?'

'I was with Schneider just now,' Levy explained in a whisper.

'Where?'

'I took a room at the Sentinel Hotel. I'm telling you: tip-top totty!'

'And she was willing to go to the hotel?'

'Never mind "willing" — it was her idea!'

'*Mazeltov!*' Ritter rose a little from the bench, thoroughly impressed, and gripped Karl's hand.

'But I'm telling you,' Levy continued with a fresh surge of enthusiasm, 'she's on fire! Ten *shiksas* I'd give you for her.'

'And Doctor Macleese?'

'What about Doctor Macleese?'

'Is there anything between them?'

'No. Now I'm sure there isn't; she despises him.'

'All the same, she's crafty …'

'She's like no one else. He won't get her! He extended our walk to an hour. We told him we were going to the cinema.' After a pause, he added, 'And the same thing tomorrow. She wants us to meet up in Vienna too, but there are some others there ...'

'All the same, don't get carried away. You need to think of your lung.'

'What has my lung got to do with it? My lung is almost healthy! There's no danger.'

'Karl, Karl, lie down!' Ritter interjected urgently. 'Doctor Macleese is on patrol.'

In the gloom Karl Levy crept to his bench, hunching the upper half of his body, and inserted himself hurriedly under the blankets. When Doctor Macleese approached Levy's bench, he was lying there as if nothing had happened.

'Just arrived, Herr Levy?' the doctor asked.

'What do you mean? I came back half an hour ago, at six.'

'What did you see at the cinema?'

'It was jolly good.'

'What was showing there?'

'They were showing... I've forgotten the title... Aha! I remember now: *The Lost Bride*.'

The sky was clear and deep again, and the sun blazed. Everything was clean, the ground still wet from the rain of recent days, and an invigorating freshness was diffused through the warm and polished air. The gigantic mountains felt closer, although the snow abounded in their crevices and in places as far as the foothills.

The patients of the sanatorium inhaled with relief. Once more they went out for walks, arranged engagements, took photographs, conspired and intrigued, as usual.

After lunch Greta Finger came across Ornik in the corridor and asked how he was.

Ornik replied, somewhat embarrassed, 'So-so. Same as usual.'

'Are you going out at four?'

'I don't know yet. Possibly … perhaps … and the lady?'

'Of course! I always go.'

After that Ornik lay on his bench and reached a firm decision not to go out at four. Better to lie down for an hour, especially as his temperature was high today. He had to be more careful! Walking did no good at all. He would go out when he wasn't feeling so hot.

At a quarter to four, when all the others rose and began preparing to leave, Ornik remained supine. He took out the thermometers from his mouth and his armpit and found a reading of 37.3 — he couldn't possibly go out! He also felt weary, and his head was heavy.

When the sound of the gong resounded through the corridors and the inmates hurried to their four o'clock snack, Ornik got up slowly, closed the grey booth that was his personal shelter, patiently folded the blankets, went into his room, washed his hands and face and rinsed out his mouth as usual, and then started walking down slowly to the dining room.

On the stairs he stopped for a moment, as if meeting an invisible barrier. Then he turned and went back up the stairs hastily, distractedly, took his coat and hat from the wardrobe in the corridor, and hurried down again.

Ornik consumed his cocoa in big gulps, in a state of utter abstraction, and went out immediately to put his shoes on.

In the corridor stood Greta Finger, with her shoes on, ready to go out.

'What is this — you're going out after all, Herr Ornik?' said Greta with the ghost of a smile, and turned while speaking to Seberg, who had emerged just then from the boot room: 'Let's go, Herr Engineer!'

For a moment, Ornik remained in his place as if rooted there. It seemed to him that both his thighs had seized up simultaneously, and a wave of warmth suddenly flooded his whole body. Nevertheless, he went into the boot room, which was already almost empty, and started putting on his shoes. Midway through the process he changed his mind and took them off again. Better to lie down at this hour and not put any strain on his lung! But even while thinking this thought he was putting his shoes on once more. Ornik left the sanatorium and headed straight for the casino, yes indeed: his legs were entirely beyond their master's control and took him there on their own initiative.

In the spacious hall — two long walls consisting solely of big windows, set side by side, and a vaulted ceiling painted with naked cavorting nymphs from Greek mythology, and little angels, plump and round-limbed and playing ancient musical instruments — the air now hung heavy and warm, mingled with the smells of mascara and perfume and cigarette smoke. The swarthy waitresses in their white caps and ironed aprons weaved deftly between the cramped tables, laid with white cloths, the punters seated around them, occupying all the space. The tables sat between two rows of palm trees with broad green leaves, standing in big wooden tubs along the full length of the hall. The chairs lined up on both sides of the entrance door — for those who had come only to hear the music — were already all taken, and even the gallery, extending into a mezzanine floor inside the hall, was full of people.

Ornik entered and remained standing near the door. On the stage opposite him, arranged in a semicircle, the band was playing something by Wagner. Ornik's consciousness was in an utter fog. He absorbed the bright colours of the women's clothing, and the cacophonous sounds interlocking together, without any awareness on his part — he did not see or hear anything. It wasn't that he felt any kind of obtrusive sadness, or bitterness, or any other such emotion — there was not a trace of this in him. But he felt almost petrified, as if he were immobilised, so that nothing around him was perceived by his senses. He stood there as if someone had transported him from somewhere else and happened to choose this place to set him down. And thus he would stand for a long time, until somebody arrived to take him somewhere else.

During the five o'clock intermission, Greta Finger popped up in front of Ornik as if she had emerged from the ground, and with her was the engineer.

Ornik stared at her with startled eyes: he did not seem to recognise her. 'Why are you looking at me like that, Ornik?' Greta laughed. 'Don't you know me?'

'I mean … of course, I … I know you very well …' Ornik mumbled.

'Well, that is nice, very nice, knowing that you still know me. Well now' — Greta was in a hurry — 'come on, Ornik, let's go back! It's time.'

'Really, is it that time already?' Ornik peered at the clock above the stage. 'Yes, it's true! Very good … or rather, just as well that you mentioned it … I had completely forgotten …'

Ornik walked at Greta's side. What a shame they had to go back to the sanatorium already! Now, of all times, Ornik wasn't tired. Not at all. It would be good just now to walk for a while …

'You'll end up like a human being yet, Ornik!' said Seberg. 'The trick is to walk a lot and learn *how* to walk! The rest will come by itself.'

'And do you know,' Greta said with a smile, 'for a long time now I've been in love with Ornik … he's the most handsome boy in the sanatorium.'

'How is that?' said the engineer. 'I thought you were in love with Adler — I remember hearing you say that a few days ago.'

'No, that was just a joke, my heart belongs to Ornik, truly and genuinely.'

'You see, Ornik, you go out for a walk just once and you break the heart of a beautiful girl.' The engineer smiled.

But in the end, what did she want from him, this Greta Finger? Ornik wondered as they went into the sanatorium.

In the Albano Valley spring suddenly appeared. It came so stealthily that no one noticed its arrival, but then even the winter had a taste of spring to it here. In a single day the trees and shrubs started to bloom, to bloom unashamedly, and a sharp perfume wafted through the valley. The waters of the Passer, swollen by the snow that melted unseen in the mountain heights, now ran in a vigorous spate as if they were afraid of arriving late. The rains and the mists disappeared completely; in the daytime the sun blazed with renewed vigour; and even the nights were warmer now — such was the spring.

Sebag Adler made his preparations a day in advance. The plan was complete in every detail.

When he returned from the evening walk, he didn't leave his shoes in the boot room as usual, but took them up surreptitiously and hid them in the wardrobe in the corridor. Truth be told, Adler was a little more irritable than usual that evening, but no one noticed this. In the sanatorium they were all irritable all the time, more or less, but especially in the evenings.

At nine-thirty Adler stripped off his clothes and lay down. He had already taken his coat and shoes from the wardrobe, hiding them under the bed.

The room was dark. In the other bed Ritter was already lying down and, annoyingly, he didn't want to go to sleep. He talked incessantly, which irritated Adler to the point of insanity.

'... And he comes in the very moment that he's kissing her in the corridor,' Ritter told the story in an excited whisper, 'as if on purpose ... Later, Doctor Volk is shouting his head off in Richard Berlin's room, saying he won't tolerate such conduct here under any circumstances! "This is juvenile behaviour," he yells, so worked up that his eyes are watering. "Juvenile behaviour, which has no place *in a sanatorium*! This isn't an amusement park for naughty children, but a place for serious and decent people who only want to be nursed back to health!" et cetera, et cetera. But Richard Berlin isn't keeping quiet. He, Berlin that is, won't let anyone interfere in his private affairs. He is not a "naughty child" and Doctor Volk should be a little more circumspect in his choice of words. He abides by the rules of the sanatorium no less than the other patients, definitely no less, and he takes appropriate care of his health. If his conduct is so disagreeable in the eyes of the doctor, he's prepared to leave the sanatorium tomorrow, tomorrow morning. Doctor Volk could use his time more profitably in learning how to deal with sick people. In his capacity as a doctor he should know that any agitation, however mild, is harmful to lung patients, and this should be the focus of his attention! On hearing this the doctor lowers his voice and starts to apologise, saying that he meant no offence, but "Herr Berlin must surely realise for himself that this is not the place for such things ... the founders and benefactors of the institution did not have such purposes in mind; they wanted to give unfortunate invalids the opportunity to regain their health."'

When will this idiot shut up? Adler thought angrily. *This of all evenings he doesn't want to sleep!*

'And he's expelled Lyuba Goldis separately,' Ritter continued. 'She's crying now in her room. And tomorrow they must both leave the sanatorium. They have been told.'

Adler's nerves were close to breaking point. He could go to this Ritter right now and strangle him, strangle him without pity, anything to shut him up.

Adler did not make a sound. He pretended to be asleep. For some moments now he had no longer been taking in Ritter's words. He heard only the aggravating whisper, constantly burbling away in the darkness.

At long last Ritter fell asleep. He started snoring: isolated snores at first, mild and sporadic, and gradually taking on greater force, like a whole chorus.

Adler lay still for a while and listened to his neighbour's snores. His mind was now completely clear.

Tomorrow I might be in another place … The idea flashed in his head.

In the distant night, the tower-clock chimed, twice. Ten-thirty already.

Adler lifted himself and sat up carefully in the bed, listening for a moment, stretched out a hand towards the chair, which was completely hidden in the darkness, and slowly picked up his trousers. Suddenly the bed creaked — *curses!* For a moment Adler froze; it seemed to him that Ritter's snoring had stopped. But no, he was asleep as before. Adler started to fiddle with his trousers, struggling to put them on and not succeeding. *What is wrong with these trousers? They've gone mad, mad and useless …* Aha — it became clear to Adler, after exhaustive probing, that he had inserted his right leg into the left trouser leg and his left leg into the right. What a time to do it! He almost burst into laughter: what an obstacle course this was proving to be. He would have to take the bloody trousers off and put them on again.

Sweating profusely, Adler finally succeeded, after a long time and with many pauses, in putting on all his clothes. He got down from the bed and stood and listened. Then he bent down and took out his coat and shoes from under the bed.

In his socks Adler moved towards the door and put his ear to it. The corridor was quiet. He reached for the handle and here it came — his flesh crawled — but no, it was the tower-clock starting to peal. Blessed be the tower-clock, for standing by Adler when he opened the door.

The corridor was dimly lit, and the absolute emptiness was a little scary. Adler stopped for a moment to catch his breath. His eyes were somewhat dazzled by the sudden transition into the light. There was a heavy, compressed silence in the corridor.

He started going down the stairs with furtive steps in his socks, his coat and shoes held in his hand. Outside the door of Room 17 on the lower floor, Fleischmann and Kisch's room, Adler paused, listened for a while, then cautiously opened the door and went in.

In the room there was silence. But beside the glass door opposite, open to the balcony, Adler could just make out a large human shape in the gloom. A shudder passed through him, and then he remembered: this must be Fleischmann, waiting for him as arranged.

Holding his breath, and with great effort, Adler crossed the big room, past the sleeping Kisch, and the two youths went out onto the balcony. They sat on one of the nearest benches to put their shoes on, without a word said. Despite this, Adler could hear, or sense, the intense and accelerated beating of his heart.

Then they climbed over the balustrade of the balcony, let themselves down onto the plinth on the other side, and from there jumped down into the garden.

Once they had cautiously left the garden, where the sand and gravel crunched mercilessly under their feet, they remained standing outside, close to the gate. For some time they were silent, needing to regain their strength after their exertion. There was not a soul around. The night was chilly and clear. Adler took a foldable hat from his coat pocket and stuck it on his head.

'Perhaps they won't come at all,' Adler whispered to his companion.

'No, they are definitely coming!' the other answered confidently.

What a dirty old goat I am! Adler chided himself inwardly. *A Jew who has already gone through thirty years of exertion and upheaval, and still he maintains his evil ways.* 'Maybe it wouldn't be so bad if they have changed their minds.'

'No! They haven't changed their minds.'

The door of the clinic opened and closed again. They pressed themselves flat against the fence and hid under the shadow of the trees with outspread branches.

Footsteps approached and two women came out through the garden gate.

'There, there they are!' said Fleischmann, and he called out in a whisper: 'Betty!'

The women came closer.

'Let's go!' Betty whispered with a hint of panic. They directed their steps silently towards the Obermais.

When they reached the main highway, some distance from the sanatorium, the four of them, as if they had planned it, suddenly burst into loud, uninhibited laughter, breaking up and soaring into the black wasteland of the night.

'Ha-ha-ha!' Annie held her belly with both hands and rocked the upper half of her body forward and back. 'Ha-ha-ha! I can't stand any more of this! Ha-ha-ha!'

It was strange, this laughter of the four people in the middle of the night, by the banks of the gurgling Passer, strange and intimidating, and suddenly Adler was frightened by his own mirth and that of his companions. Rising to the forefront of his imagination were tales of high-spirited heroes grabbing their heart's desire on nights of horror; of beautiful young women casting spells and trapping innocent young men, transporting them thousands of leagues away to join in their wild orgies.

'Well, let's go, children!' urged Betty.

Their route stretched a little way along the shore, before the luxurious Grand Hotel, its many windows now with their blinds drawn, and then veered to the right, alongside the turreted Gothic church, which stood silent, black, and self-contained. They passed the little garden of trees and turned left. The steep streets of the Obermais were dark, as the streetlamps had already been extinguished. But here and there twinkled the isolated light of a lit window or a tavern.

The single saloon of the little tavern, which the two couples entered, was bathed in semi-darkness. Its walls were panelled halfway up from the base with smooth dark-brown wood, which had turned black over the years. From the wooden veneer to the vaulted ceiling, in every space not occupied by the cheap paintings — old, smoke-stained landscapes and hunting scenes, already full of innumerable cracks and the black traces left behind by flies, whose once-blue skies had already turned grey-orange — in flowing Gothic script, red letters on grey background, maxims such as this appeared:

Rebensaft
Gibt uns Kraft,
Regt das Blut,
Macht uns Mut.[*]

Dark deer-horns, large sets of antlers, entwined and interlaced, were fixed to the middle of each wall and served as coat hooks. The tables, benches, and chairs, made from hard oak, were clumsily constructed, solid, ancient, and rustic.

In the room there were only two other guests, two drunk Italian soldiers. One had his head on its side, resting on one hand, splayed to its full breadth on the table, his red face gaping in a smile, his fingers tapping wearily on the tabletop, and his grey service cap worn back to front.

[*] German: 'Wine gives us strength, rouses our blood, strengthens the heart.'

His mate sat beside him and leaned against the back of the chair, his head slumped backwards and his face to the ceiling, intoning in a rough, thick voice the lyrics of a popular Italian song. The tumblers of thick and polished glass, all empty, stood before them on the table, which was wet in places, and at the bottom of a bulbous bottle was a residue of red wine.

Upon the entry of the late guests, the tired waitress — who had been sitting beside the door to the kitchen and playing idly with a fat cat, which had irregular patches of white and grey and purred contentedly in her lap — leaped up from her place as if waking from a bad dream, and dropped the cat, which at once began flexing its forepaws.

'What are the gentlemen ordering?' she asked in a voice gummed up by sleep. The newcomers were already sitting down at the table in the corner.

Adler ordered two litres of their best red wine.

'Well then, Annie.' Adler held her by her soft chin and smiled into her eyes. 'Whom do you love more, me or Hansel?

'Which Hansel?' Annie was taken by surprise.

'No doubt Herr Adler is referring to Herman,' Betty explained.

'Oh, Herman! Well, the two of you equally … right now it's you, you alone!' Annie winked at him with her mocking eyes and tried to tickle him under his arms.

Adler was fired up. He wound both his arms around her body, pressed himself with all his strength against her full breasts, and bit her lip until it bled.

'Ow!' cried Annie, her face reddened by emotion. 'That hurts, my treasure!'

They filled the glasses, made a toast 'to life', emptied them, and filled them again.

Their hearts were merry from the heavy, slightly sweet wine of South Tyrol. Annie's clumsy thigh was already curled around Adler's and scorched it like fire. She took the big glasses from Adler's eyes and perched them on her nose.

'Look, I'm a professor!' she giggled, as happy as a little girl. 'Like the one who's staying at the Hotel Continental.'

It was already after midnight. The older soldier rose heavily and pulled his comrade after him, and the two of them staggered outside, clinging together and swaying this way and that, like ears of corn in the wind.

'Time to go!' Adler said, his domed forehead already red to the roots of his hair, and his eyes flashing like glass.

Adler was hot, and as he rose, he felt an excessive lightness in his body, as if the earth's gravitational force had lessened a little. The tall Fleischmann was chuckling away all the time and needed no excuse.

Outside, the cold wrapped around their blazing faces and restored their spirits a little, like a cool, dim cellar on a hot summer's day.

Annie leaned full and soft on Adler. She thrust the hand that was entwined with his into his coat pocket, and their fingers interlocked.

Adler's mind was buoyant, immeasurably so. All the twisted things in him had been straightened, and a fiery joie de vivre flooded his whole being. He was aware of a powerful impulse to break into song, a lively song, the kind that delights the spirit.

Betty's room, which she rented out regularly, in an old two-storey house in the Obermais, wasn't far away. Betty opened the door and the four of them entered a dark passageway. By the light of matches, they climbed the rickety wooden stairs to the first floor, and went into the room.

The lamp was lit, revealing a small, low-ceilinged room, meagrely furnished. The ancient wooden bed was unmade, and the blankets on top were piled up and mixed together in a heap, as if someone had got up just now, still half asleep. The pillow was crumpled and pushed to one side, and on the white sheet, no longer pristine, was a stray black feather. On the table, which was covered with old newspaper, there was a blackened knife that obviously hadn't been wiped after use, along with an orange slice, already shrivelled with a white crust. The air was heavy and dense, several days old.

Adler immediately opened the window and let in a little of the night air. Then he pulled Annie down onto the battered, lumpy sofa, which stood at the foot of the bed.

'Wait a moment,' she whispered, her breath hot.

With quick and clumsy movements she removed her broad-brimmed hat, made of black felt with a garland of flowers and leaves, stripped off her black coat and her thick blouse with its black and white stripes, and her heavy breasts pressed through the ungainly nightgown.

At four in the morning, tired and still bleary from sleep, the two couples made their way back, traversing the drowsy town from end to end. Heads empty of thought and knees shaky, they moved slowly and lazily, their footsteps absorbed by the opaque night and mingling with a few early cockcrows, which stopped and started again.

Before the garden of the sanatorium they parted, and the two men went back the way they had come. All had gone smoothly.

Afterwards, in his own bed, Adler slept a heavy, dreamless sleep, as if his head had been cut off.

'Seven-thirty already!' Ritter roused Adler the next morning. 'The breakfast gong will be going off any moment now!'

'What?' Adler awoke, alarmed and not knowing at first where he was. His nose was dried out from the inside and refreshed by an agreeable sleep and by the cool air filtering in through the open door, and his head was heavy with a slight ache. Little by little he perked up and remembered the events of the previous night, which now seemed totally unreal.

He dressed and washed in a hurry. On his way down for a late breakfast, he met the superintendent in the corridor and wished her a civil good morning. Short and squat, she stood facing him, blocking his way, and said in a matter-of-fact manner, her face expressionless but her sharp eyes piercing like needles, 'Herr Adler is leaving the sanatorium today.'

'Who?' Adler had no idea what she was talking about.

It was he, Herr Adler, she repeated in a soft voice, not taking her eyes from him. Herman would bring him his luggage and he would pack his possessions.'

'How can that be?' Adler tried his luck. 'I'm supposed to be here for two more weeks!'

Correct, but this was an exceptional case, and the full term of his treatment would not be completed, since they here were not prepared to tolerate nocturnal excursions like those of Herr Adler. They designated two hours each day for recreational walking, which was quite enough for sick people.'

'Is that everything?' said Adler, moving on to the dining room.

The dining room was already empty, and Paula was busy clearing away the cups and the empty cake baskets from the tables.

How did this come to light? The question drilled into Adler's brain as he absently chewed the fresh cakes and sipped the tepid, tasteless cocoa.

The fact itself did not distress him unduly. The sanatorium experience had been anathema to him since the very first day. The communal living and the prison-style regime, which he could under no circumstances get used to, grated on his nerves more and more every day. Even the faces of the different patients, with the seal of death on them, were beginning to irritate him more than he could stand; he did not need to be reminded at every turn of his own inevitable mortality. And in recent weeks he had wondered on several occasions if he wouldn't be better off going back to Vienna before his time was up, although there was no doubt that he still needed therapy, and his stay in the sanatorium had definitely improved the state of his lung. Anyway, the loss of two weeks in the sanatorium was a price worth paying for that adventure, not for the business itself, but for the subterfuge, the fear, and the tension bound up with it. And yet in spite of everything, the idea of being ordered to leave didn't appeal to him now.

In any case, Adler went to his room and started focusing on his return to Vienna. The patients were already lying on the balconies. Rumours of the 'night trip' had spread rapidly through the building. Everyone knew everything, and on all four balconies they whispered about nothing else. How did it get out? It was a mystery to Adler.

Ritter called to Adler through the open door. 'How did you do it?' he asked with a laugh. 'How did you manage to do it without anyone knowing?'

'You can see for yourself that everybody knows!'

'But I sleep next to you in the same room, in the bed next to yours, and I noticed nothing. Congratulations, Herr Adler! Our own robber baron, a title richly deserved — congratulations! What a shame I didn't know anything about your powers until it was too late.'

Adler moved among the recumbent patients like a free man, no longer being made to rest. He felt like a boy expelled from school, sauntering along the streets, hands in his pockets.

'Wonderful, Herr Adler,' young Windel congratulated him, his bulging eyes threatening to leap from their sockets out of sheer delight. 'Very nice! Not like these maggots, who lie around here and swallow their own spit. You're one of us: long live Brigittenau, Vienna!'

Herman brought in Adler's two brown suitcases from

the lift. His watery blue eyes glanced at Adler insolently, and a malicious half-smile flickered on his face.

Aha! A sudden flash ignited in Adler's brain. *The janitor! He was the one who opened the door for the women last night, and it's pretty obvious he's the one who grassed on them ...*

The train departed from Albano at two p.m. At twelve-thirty his possessions were already packed and stowed in the corridor downstairs. Adler had paid his outstanding debts in the office and was now eating lunch by himself, before the other patients, so he wouldn't be late for the train. He ate without much appetite, as was usual before a journey, leaving most of the food uneaten and finishing quickly. On leaving the dining room he met Kisch, who was loitering hungrily in the corridor.

Kisch asked innocently, 'Not hungry yet, Herr Adler? Lunch is even later than usual today. My stomach is rumbling for food!'

'I've already eaten, Herr Kisch,' Adler replied with a smile.

'You've already eaten? Must have been to a restaurant in town. I myself sometimes stop for a snack there during our walks, when the hunger is most oppressive ... Here's an adage for you, Herr Adler: a man will always eat the moment his appetite is aroused!'

'Not in town, Herr Kisch; I ate here, in the dining room.'

'How did you manage that? Sounds like corruption to me: bribery will get you anywhere! I've noticed that you seem to have special privileges here in the sanatorium ... I tell you Herr Adler, bribery is the biggest thing in the world; it works everywhere and at all times!'

'Corruption, to be sure.' Adler smiled. 'I'm going to Vienna today!'

'Wha-a-at?' Kisch narrowed his little eyes in feigned astonishment and peered sidelong at his interlocutor. 'No, you're having me on!'

'No, no, Herr Kisch, I really am going today.'

'Impossible!'

'Nevertheless ...'

'And why the hurry, Herr Adler? Surely your time here isn't even up yet. No doubt you have urgent business in Vienna, things that can't be delayed ...'

'Very true, Herr Kisch, urgent business.'

'All the same, as a true friend I advise you to stay here until your time is up. The most important thing, I tell you, is health, and the lung is the most vital organ in the human body. Listen to my advice, Herr Adler, advice drawn from age and experience: use your time wisely! It's not every day that you can go to a place of healing. Your business won't go away, I tell you; stay until your term is finished. You could even ask for an extra month! They'll give you an extension. You, they are bound to give it to you!'

'I have to go today.' Adler smiled. 'I can't delay!'

'Well,' Kisch pouted his fleshy lips with an air of resignation, 'if your decision is irrevocable, I won't try to persuade you. My duty, my fraternal duty, I have discharged ... but I shall tell you one more time —'

'Goodbye, Herr Kisch,' Adler interrupted him, and held out his hand in farewell.

'Goodbye and bon voyage! It would be a great honour

to meet you in Vienna. I invite you to visit me at my home, Herr Adler! You will drink good black coffee in my house, the very best — in all Vienna you will find no coffee to rival it! My address: Hahngasse 24, in the ninth district. Don't forget!'

'Yes, I shall call on you as soon as I find the time.'

Kisch clutched Adler's hand again.

'Well, goodbye and all the best to you, Herr Kisch!' Adler finally retrieved his hand and turned to go up to the first floor.

'Bon voyage! You would do me a great honour, Herr Adler! My compliments! I'm relying on you, sir,' Kisch called out behind Adler. 'It will be a great delight for me. Hahngasse 24, don't forget, and ask for Herr Arnold Kisch. Add the Arnold! In this house there is one other Kisch ...'

Bad days came upon Ornik, days of worry and confusion. All his free time was no longer sufficient for him to take proper care of his diseased lung, which demanded so much treatment. Some obscure little screw had come loose, and the whole of the Ornik machine had stopped operating its daily routine of temperature checks, of rest, of caution, and all the rest. Admittedly, he was lying down now for the stipulated time, like the other patients, but this was no longer genuine, beneficial rest. In his repose now there was none of the required intention, or the desirable inner tranquillity; there was no diminution of awareness: this wasn't rest for its own sake.

Ornik's internal organs were now in constant turmoil, losing patience. Something irksome, totally concealed from his consciousness, was rebelling against the way of life that he had imposed upon himself, as endorsed by the institution, since the day he fell ill. He was lying on his bench in a perturbed state, waiting impatiently for the end of resting time. Ornik was treating himself with utter disregard. He no longer paid close attention to the processes operating inside him, his temperature chart was carelessly maintained, he was raising his voice without being aware of it, and he didn't miss a single walk. This Ornik, one could say, had turned into a different Ornik.

And it was strange the way that the former pains had really stopped, or at least he wasn't conscious of them. Even his teeth, which used to plague him endlessly, had decided to behave themselves and were leaving him alone. It seemed his face had changed too. It was now more open, less immobile, and instead of its habitual turbid pallor had taken on a healthier colour.

Ornik was going for walks with Greta Finger on a regular basis. He accompanied her to the shops, waiting patiently and willingly while she made her purchases, and then effortlessly carrying the parcels as a matter of course, laughing at the girl's gibes, and not noticing as the allocated walking time elapsed. Indeed, this single hour of walking was now too short for Ornik. He could have walked, if only it were allowed, for many hours, even all day.

The boys would tease him about Greta Finger, mocking him in good humour, but Ornik smiled a private smile to himself, or sometimes replied with a witticism of his own.

Everything seemed to be good. But this Greta Finger

was stuck in Ornik like a bone in the throat. He was incapable of understanding the girl's mind. He knew nothing of her personality, or what her attitude was towards him. But he thought it was important to know this, and Ornik wearied his brain to no end, on his bench in the daytime, or lying awake at night, analysing every word, every remark of hers, and coming up with nothing.

One mild night in early April, Ornik lay in bed, his eyes wide open to the darkness. It was already past midnight, and Ornik's spirit was fully awake. He had no hope of sleeping tonight, but he felt at ease with this. All kinds of thoughts, dissipated and bound together, wandered around him in the dim void, fragments of past and present and even things that never were. In the spacious parlour of his parents' home, the sun of a summer afternoon was shining. Silence, and just a hint of soporific boredom. Alfred, his younger brother, still a toddler, only reached up as far as Ornik's knees. Ornik bent down now and then, from his full height, took the child by the leg and lifted him off the floor, the way one might lift a chair holding one of the legs, and the infant curled up with laughter. Black Ilonka, the neighbour's daughter, climbed up and sat in Ornik's lap, laughing merrily, kissing him on the tip of his nose, on his pursed lips and his earlobe, running her splayed fingers, thin and long, through his black hair, suddenly burying her head in his chest and starting to sob quietly, and when Ornik lifted her face he found the little liar grinning through her tears and saying that he, Ornik, was a very bad man, the baddest of them all.

Amid these images, Seberg's bed creaked from time to time as he turned over. Peeking through the open glass door were the soothing night and part of the white mattress on the next bench. A cat suddenly wailed in the distance, a frightened, blood-curdling wail, like the sound of a crying baby, blending into the black night.

Ornik now knew for certain that he would find it impossible to detach himself from her, and this thought did not upset him at all. In his head he talked to her passionately.

He had no inclination to play the fool, in the manner of the youths today, he said, why didn't she want to believe him?

She knew, Greta Finger replied. She was well acquainted with Ornik.

Did she see, all the time he hadn't wanted to talk. Hadn't she known it all without his saying anything? He'd wanted to wait, to test himself. He couldn't let go of her. Most precious of all things to him — why didn't she believe it?

No, she believed, but —

All his life was in her hands — Ornik was afraid of letting her finish — he would do anything she commanded him to do! Was she smiling? Let her despise him to her heart's content, if it gave her pleasure. He didn't care! But he couldn't give her up. And even if she didn't love him he didn't mind. So long as she walked with him, so long as she didn't abandon him.

On the contrary, said Greta solemnly, she did not despise him in the least; she had never despised him. He was very dear to her, Ornik. But she was afraid there wasn't —

He would go with her to Prague, said a heated Ornik, to Vienna or to any place she chose! The state of his health would improve too. It was getting better all the time. She could see for herself that he no longer had any ailments! He was almost completely cured ...

He was clearly making progress and she was very pleased to see this. With all her heart she was delighted. But she knew she was no good for him; she knew herself well enough. Ornik needed a completely different kind of girl. A quieter girl. She, Greta, was too turbulent, volatile. Besides, Greta concluded with a smile, she was already betrothed ...

So there it was — she was betrothed. He had indeed heard something like this, but he didn't believe it ... So she really was betrothed, but in spite of this, there was nothing to it! A very small detail ... and where was the fiancé?

In Prague.

No, this was no hindrance at all! Just an everyday thing ... it could be cancelled so easily! He was now almost completely healthy! He'd go to Prague and talk to her mother ... he'd go tomorrow! He'd kneel before her and beg. Her mother would definitely accept him ... definitely, definitely ... her mother had a compassionate heart. He was already cured! He couldn't do without Greta, he didn't care, he couldn't ... he was already healthy ...

Ornik went on talking to Greta Finger with a seething, sorrowful heart, running short of breath. In the meantime it started to turn grey outside with the dawn twilight, before changing to blue-green. Suddenly Ornik found himself walking over a snow-covered winter landscape, a large and alien expanse, a place that he did not know. Ornik had already been walking for some time and he was now very tired, his strength running out, sapped by painful fatigue; he had to sit down and rest a while, but there was no house anywhere round here and nowhere to sit. The journey was urgent: his whole life was bound up in this walking. The cold was intense, but he was warm — at least he was warm, Ornik consoled himself. But suddenly his left ear started to bother him: he felt stabbing pains in it, coming from outside and intensifying as he walked on. Ornik rubbed his ear and found it had swollen, growing so large that it occupied the whole side of his head. It was because of the cold — Ornik explained it to himself at once, and the thing was absolutely obvious to him, but it dawned on him that now all was lost, beyond recovery. Despite this he carried on walking with the last of his strength, and every step magnified the pain in his ear as if he were treading on it, to the point where he no longer felt his former weariness. Ornik suddenly remembered a remedy. How strange that he hadn't recalled this simple remedy straight away. He needed a woman to hit the swollen ear with a stick, hit it with all her strength, and then it would return to normal and the pain would stop. But there was no woman around. The stabbing became unbearably sharp. Ornik was already walking very slowly, as the left ear was oppressing him like a heavy load, bending him down to the ground: any moment now he would fall — and then all would be lost forever! And then from a distance he saw a person approaching. Yes, it was a woman, Ornik noticed as she came closer, and luckily for him she had a stick too! Now everything could be put right. When the space between them was no more than a few paces, Ornik saw that the woman was very old, stooped, and limping. Her head was wrapped in a black shawl. One eye was blind, closed and sunk deep in the socket, and the other — a black eye without any white at all, projecting from her face, and with a sharp point like a nail. The old woman stood before Ornik, leaning on her short stick, her mouth gaping in a toothless laugh and her nail-eye pointing towards him. The pain in his ear stopped for a moment of its own accord. Ornik probed it once again with his fingers, but it was as swollen as before. He knew the pain hadn't stopped for long and it would come back at any moment, but Ornik was shy for some reason about asking the old woman to hit him with the stick — it seemed indecent. Besides, she would surely fall over when she raised the stick she was leaning on. Before Ornik could change his mind, the old woman understood on her own what was needed, and she raised her stick and hit the ear once and once again. Ah! Ornik felt it. But this was his mother — it dawned on him suddenly — where had she got that stick from? How strange! The old woman went on raising the stick time and again, and hitting him, and her empty mouth laughed a black laugh, and Ornik felt more and more at ease. The pain even became a strange sort of pleasure. And meanwhile, the old woman doing the hitting was no longer his mother but Greta Finger in a long black dress, laughing and whacking him with a sheer stocking. In the middle of all this, Seberg the engineer stood up and laughed maliciously, saying: *Well done, Fräulein Greta! Whack him hard enough and he'll become a human being!* But Ornik felt a great sense of pleasure, which increased with every blow, a pleasure such as he had never felt before —

'Well, Ornik, aren't you getting up today?' Seberg roused him, standing beside Ornik's bed in his shirtsleeves and soaping his face for a shave.

'What's the time?' Ornik opened his eyes, and he felt as if he hadn't slept at all.

'Eight-thirty already!' the engineer lied cheerfully, and carried on soaping himself. 'You've missed breakfast!'

Still lying down, Ornik stretched out his hand to the night-table and picked up his watch. A quarter to eight. Still, it was time to get up. He lay there for a while longer, feeling a moment of intense fatigue, as if after a stupendous exertion. And then he raised himself and took his socks from the chair beside him, put one of them on, and remained seated, hunched up on the bed; and with the other sock in his hand he made an effort to remember something very important. A moment ago he had known for a fact there was something he had to do. What was it he needed to do? Ornik probed his left ear. Nonsense: it was only a dream! But what did he need to do? What was it? Aha — Ornik found it suddenly — he had to shave; his beard was sprouting. And while thinking this thought, Ornik had already forgotten all about shaving. *The old woman had a strange eye!* he thought, smiling to himself. *And she didn't speak at all, just laughed with her black mouth. In fact, you never hear a voice in a dream, not an explicit voice! Perhaps under hypnosis.* Ornik went on dressing slowly, stopping from time to time, then remembering and starting again. Before the mirror hanging above the white enamel basin, by the glass door to the balcony, Seberg stood tall and lean, scraping his thin cheek with a mechanical shaver, scraping one place hastily and repeatedly. Ornik glanced over there and absently caught in the mirror the scrawny knuckles of the engineer, who had wearied of the mechanical apparatus. *In spite of this he's still too fat, Seberg the engineer*, Ornik thought to himself this uncharitable thought. *It's all in vain! Yes, it's all in vain …* The last three words lodged obstinately in Ornik's brain like three heavy weights, and they refused to leave. *All in vain! What is all in vain?* Ornik had forgotten the beginning of the thought, and he turned the words over in his head without knowing what they meant: *all, a-a-all in vain!*

'The gong's going off any moment now, Ornik. Why are you sitting there like a zombie?' the engineer urged him. His face was purple from the shaving, and he was using a towel to clean the dismantled shaver parts.

'Yes, yes …' muttered Ornik distractedly. 'Of course … a-a-all … that is, we should … yes, we should …'

Ornik was finally dressed, and he approached the basin to wash. He forgot to rinse out his mouth first, his old habit, and began at once to wash his hands with great deliberation, as if they were the essential part of the process, and after this he wiped his dry face, which he had forgotten to wash. He then wandered back and forth and looked for things that were there before his eyes. In the course of the search he forgot what he was looking for and why; and finally, a quarter of an hour after the gong had sounded, he went down unshaven to the dining room.

Thereafter Ornik's mind became ever more turbid; he was more silent than usual that day, and gave the impression of being sorely troubled. There were important issues here, weighty things that turned over in his mind without a pause, demanding serious consideration, since Ornik felt clearly that his entire existence depended only on them, on these obscure things, but all his efforts to remember them, to understand their nature, availed him nothing. Every time he almost managed to grasp them — and it seemed that in another moment he would understand them fully — they slipped from his memory yet again and disappeared. Ornik struggled and struggled to remember, and his mind became more and more deranged. He was like someone wandering in the murky darkness, walking in circles around his home and not finding it.

When Doctor Macleese approached his bench at ten o'clock, Ornik didn't notice him at all. The doctor picked up the temperature chart from the chair, glanced at it, and asked Ornik why he hadn't recorded his temperature today.

'What?' Ornik stared at him with demented eyes. Temperature? He forgot … that is, yes, he forgot … of course he forgot …

And how did Ornik feel in himself?

He forgot … yes … Ornik smiled to himself. Aha! How did he feel in himself? Meaning health? Yes … good! Excellent … yes, excellent!

Doctor Macleese moved on with a smile to the other benches.

Towards evening that day, Ornik went for a walk with Greta Finger. The sun had been roasting the valley all day, and now, although the sun was on the verge of setting, the air was still overheated, and walking was tiring. They crossed into Gilf Promenade, and turned to the Tappeinerweg, which rose on a winding course on the most precipitous of the slopes, a height from which one could see a sizeable section of the town and the market, and the houses piled up on top of one another right under one's feet.

Immersed in obstinate silence, Ornik walked beside the girl. Greta Finger was saying nothing this time either, unlike her normal self. Ornik's reticence had finally begun to annoy her: this big man, who walked beside her like a silent slab of rock, was an oppressive presence; and an inexplicable fear began to gnaw at her internal organs.

Why is he so stubbornly silent, as if he's being paid for it! 'Say something, Ornik!' Greta's voice had a slight tremor to it.

'Oh, yes! Of course … that is … what is there here to talk about …' Ornik mumbled as he walked on, and he smiled a mournful smile to himself, for some unknown reason.

But Greta Finger's fear was growing stronger. She felt a choking in her throat. Where did it come from, this irrational fear? Fear of whom and of what? She took no notice of Ornik's stumbling reply; she heard only his deep voice, which seemed to her strange, alien, as if coming from afar, and her inner agitation was growing even stronger. When a moment later she remembered his words, she realised that that was all they were — words upon words, with no connection between one and the next.

'Black from end to end!' The statement emerged from Ornik's mouth, although he seemed unaware of it.

'Wh-what?' Greta was scared now, and her grey-green eyes opened wide. 'No, I can't take any more of this!' she said in panic, and grabbed Ornik's arm. 'Let's go back!'

Ornik didn't hear her.

'We're going back, go-o-ing back!' the girl almost shrieked, and she pulled Ornik's hand, shocked by the sound of her own voice.

'Of course, of course …' Ornik agreed. 'What did you say, going back, yes, yes, we're going back …'

They set off on the return journey, not walking but running. Greta Finger ran as if fleeing from someone, fleeing and pulling the giant Ornik along behind her; he was taking broad paces, his eyes fixed on the ground and his big hands hanging listlessly at his sides like the broken bones of a gigantic creature.

Before they reached the garden of the sanatorium, Greta Finger stopped, drenched in sweat and short of breath. She was afraid to look at Ornik's face, and he turned to stare at her, deranged eyes sparkling with a strange fire.

'I'm going,' he said, as if talking to himself, 'yes, yes, I'm going. There's still time…'

He held out his big palm and took Greta's hand. He clutched it for a moment in his, changed his mind suddenly, bent over it, and kissed its back, a fleeting kiss. Then he turned and strode away towards the town, turned his head once more to glance, from a few paces away, at the girl who was still standing there, stunned, and he disappeared behind the fence of the Hotel Continental garden.

Ornik walked briskly, retracing the route he had followed just a few moments before with Greta Finger, completely unaware. He was filled with something heavy and large, with no definable shape, which impelled him onwards involuntarily. Ornik was walking in accordance with a blind decision, made for him by somebody else, and he had no idea what it was. But he had the vague feeling that his whole body was contracting into a dense ball of formidable energy, as if he were supposed to uproot a mountain and fling it into the Passer.

Suddenly he found himself on the Devil's Stage: a small, square wooden platform, surrounded by a railing on three sides, bridging the deep gully, above the foaming cataract of the Passer. Ornik wondered for a moment: *Which path leads to this place?* and again he forgot it at once. A haughty raven had meanwhile taken up residence among the trees on the slope, and was peering curiously at the empty Devil's Stage and the big man who stood in the middle of it without moving, as if rooted there. The trill of a solitary bird emerged from hiding and joined the frantic thrashing of the waterfall below. *A bird!* Ornik's mind cleared for a moment.

He approached the benches, meaning to sit on one of them, but changed direction and went and stood by the platform railing, leaning his chest against it and looking down, at the water crashing against the pillars of stone and sending up foam.

That stone at the side — an irrelevant thought flashed up — *looks completely smooth, and yet it makes that little cascade bounce off at an angle: it doesn't dare to climb up and over ... so simple to climb up, and yet ...* His mind was in chaos again, and Ornik struggled in vain to catch the thread of his thoughts.

There's no time! He heard someone whisper inside him.

No, no, there's no time, of course ... Ornik agreed, and a twisted smile fluttered over his lips. But Ornik didn't know why there was no time.

At that moment his crumpled black hat fell from his head, turned in the air, and disappeared into the depths below. A brief shiver passed through his body, and he felt he was being lifted off the ground from behind, suspended in inertia, before plummeting into the deep chasm — a swift and sudden fall, as in a dream. As he fell, his mind cleared for a split-second, and Ornik saw before him a double vision: the white foam of the water, and the black, dish-shaped hat of Greta Finger. Then his round head hit the rocks with a heavy thud. The Devil's Stage remained empty and disappeared into the grey twilight.

That evening the sanatorium was in uproar, with much urgent running up and down the stairs. The super-intendent bustled around, anxious and preoccupied, her blotchy, bony face displaying even more than the usual malice. The two janitors, Herman and Fridel, had already been sent for the third time into town to search for Ornik. In the corridors the inmates were gathered in groups, whispering and speculating to one another, although nobody knew anything. Doctor Volk arrived from the town in a panic, summoned by telephone, and he and Doctor Macleese ran up the stairs, both of them sweating, with Sister Lisl following close behind. Seberg the engineer was interviewed by the doctors, and Greta Finger was questioned too, but their answers revealed nothing.

The following morning Ornik was brought in and laid in the corridor, flat out on a bench. His clothes were torn and crumpled, wet, and in places stained with orange mud. From the trouser-leg, torn and folded upwards, one leg protruded, visible to the calf; a blue and hairy leg, with the sock falling down and trailing around the shoe. His brain tissue was pulp, his face stained with a mixture of congealed blood, hair, peeled skin, and dirt. The one eye that remained in place was half closed, and through its aperture a strand of albumen was visible. His fists were bruised and clenched, the left hand hanging loosely along the bench and the right laid on his chest, as if about to insert a thermometer under his armpit …

The janitor came and spread a blanket over him.

On all the balconies they suddenly knew he had been brought in. Now the patients were silent; there was nothing to add. Greta Finger lay on a bench on the third floor, her eyes fixed on some distant point, her heart constricted by intense pain, and her right hand, the hand that Ornik had leaned over the previous day and had kissed before departing, was on fire, blazing away on its own, beyond her control.

Paris, 1926

FACING THE SEA

This translation is dedicated to Esther Silverstone

Madame Bremon said, 'Make yourselves at home. There's no one here all day.' Her wrinkled face seemed smaller beneath her wide-brimmed straw hat. She stopped washing the linen by the garden wall. In the room that she showed them, a hot, viscous darkness had settled, because the shutters had been closed for so long. Adolph Barth kept wiping his forehead. 'Anyway, you're facing the sea. Twenty yards. Go! Out with you, Bijou!' She scolded the bleary-eyed black-and-white spotted puppy that was entangled between her feet.

'Yes, we are facing the sea.' Adolph Barth and his companion exchanged whispers. 'It's good enough. We'll stay.'

Towards evening, when the heat had passed, they brought over their suitcases from the train station. The sea was spread out in its richest blue. Fishermen drifted from the shore, spreading their nets from boats scattered here and there across the horizon. In the garden nearby, the tables were set for supper.

Gina lay back languorously on a colourful beach towel. She wore a light-green cotton bathing suit that accentuated her shapeliness. A flowered Chinese parasol, planted in the ground behind her, blossomed above her head. Next to her, Barth, in sunglasses, fingered the searing gravel and flicked pebbles into the water.

Dull brown nets, from which wafted the acrid odour of fish and brine, were spread out to dry behind them. The air just above the ground trembled with the heat.

Cici came out of the water and sat beside them, folding his legs oriental-style. Droplets clung to his matted chest. 'The water is warm,' he said, with a distinctly Italian accent.

'You're shaking.'

'I've been in the water for over an hour.'

Gina rolled onto her side to face the two men. Flies hovered over a forgotten little fish, left beside a nearby boat that had been drawn out of the water.

'In three days you have managed to tan a bit, madame.' Cici's eyes wandered over the curve of her pale thighs. He moved himself closer and compared his skin, the colour of copper coins, to hers, as pale as ivory.

'No, not yet like yours,' she said. And to Barth: 'Put your hat on, or lie next to me under the umbrella.'

'So what is your real name?' asked Barth.

'Francesco Adasso. But everyone here calls me Cici.' And after a moment: 'My friend from Rome is here this morning. He is the interpreter from Cook's Travel Agency, you know. He should be here any moment now.'

'Wonderful,' joked Gina.

He offered her a yellow packet of cigarettes. Gina declined. Cici and Barth smoked, lying on their bellies with the sun warming their backs. The sea sprawled motionlessly at their feet. Only on the horizon did a boat drift, dream-like. But here, next to them, romped Stefano's brood, half-a-dozen dirty children aged two and up, giggling, screaming, and splashing water. And to the side, Latzi and Suzi were playing catch with Marcelle, a dark-skinned Lyonnaise who radiated charm and youthful vigour. The three of them looked as though they were cast of bronze.

'The girl from Lyon is very beautiful,' said Gina to no one in particular.

'She is,' Cici agreed. 'But you, madame, are much more beautiful than she.'

'Thank you!'

Barth smiled with the corner of his mouth and flicked his cigarette butt in a graceful arc. 'Suzi's lipstick seems much too pale. It doesn't go with her tan.'

'*Shiksa* taste.'

'Aside from that, she is heavy about the middle.'

'Latzi is also from Vienna,' interjected Cici.

'You mean Budapest …'

A Japanese man in his bathing suit emerged from a row of houses opposite the beach, crossed the street that ran parallel to the shore, and approached. He seemed taller than most Asians, his face more clearly outlined. Following him was his companion, a European woman wearing a robe with huge saffron blossoms, and a light-blue ribbon in her hair. She was shorter than he, and about ten years older. She struck Gina as someone who was self-assured. The Japanese man dived into the water, while his companion remained with Latzi and Suzi, who had finished playing.

'Yesterday they drank until four again.' Cici knew everyone's whereabouts here.

'At Stefano's?'

'No. At the Japanese house. A night of debauchery.'

'And you?' Barth sat up. He dried his sweaty chest and thighs, upon which the gravel had left a florid tattoo. His face was flushed, and locks of flaxen hair stuck to his forehead.

'I didn't feel like it,' replied Cici.

The interpreter from Cook's was dressed like a dandy in the season's fashion. His dark hair, glistening with grease, stuck to his scalp like a bandage. His face was smooth and bloated. He extended his left hand when Cici introduced him. His right hand, in a black glove, was a prosthesis. 'Ah! So you live in Paris. I know it like the back of my hand.'

That the interpreter knew everything *like the back of his hand* was immediately clear. He was especially familiar with foreign languages ('the arts, if you please!'). In Rome he had a friend, a Japanese poetess, evidence of whom he brought with him: a book of Japanese poems with its vertical lines, 'a gift from her'. He didn't know how to read it yet, but this Japanese fellow would teach him. It was all arranged. And the lady? Would she be willing to teach him German in exchange for an Italian 'lesson'?

The Arab, so named for his ability to imitate an Arabic accent, lived and worked with Cici, and clung to the interpreter like his right-hand man. He would punctuate the interpreter's words with nodded agreement, prepared to pounce on anyone daring to doubt them.

Gina rose to swim.

'Please. Wait while I undress.' The interpreter slid

behind the beached boat, the Arab following him. After a few minutes he re-appeared, naked. The whiteness of his skin contrasted with the tans of the others, making him look indecent. His artificial hand was left behind among his clothes; the stump of his arm was wrapped in a towel. He dropped the towel, dived into the water, and began to swim. The Arab followed close behind.

'Teach me the backstroke,' Gina said to Barth. And then: 'I was swimming behind you, but I didn't have the strength and returned. You tend to go out too far. Don't let anything happen!'

Cici swam in a circle around Gina. Breathlessly and heavily, he pumped his arms and legs, making waves. 'Look here! Move your arms and legs like this. One-two; one — now you try.'

Gina let herself go, falling back onto Barth's outstretched arms, which supported her under the water. Close by, Marcelle stood and watched. 'You don't know how to swim on your back, madame? It's simple. Here!' She dived in and showed her, laughing through shining teeth that looked like a mouse's.

'And when shall we race, Mademoiselle Marcelle?' asked Barth.

'Any time you like.'

'This afternoon, all right?'

'If I don't go to Nice.'

'You like the little one, huh?' Gina said to Barth when Marcelle turned away. And to Cici: 'Monsieur Cici, you must learn the backstroke by tomorrow, you understand?' she teased.

The interpreter and the Arab approached. The interpreter crouched down, lowering himself chin-deep in the
chest-high water. He remained in this position while he was
near them. Even so, his maimed arm twinkled beneath the
clear water. Gina and Cici were splashing each other now,
while Barth, arms outstretched like smokestacks, sailed
through the crystalline blue water. When he returned, he
reminded Gina about lunch. The sun shone directly overhead. On the main street, facing the sea, was a single row
of houses broken up by waves of glowing molten orange.
Passers-by trampled their shadows underfoot.

Stefano's grocery, three houses down the street from
Madame Bremon's guesthouse, was run by his wife — a
thin Neapolitan woman of about forty whose body had
been ravaged by childbearing and hard work. Madame
Stefano was never seen outside her territory. She always
wore the same dress, which, once white, was now grey
with dirt. Her blue-black hair, always uncombed, hung in
tangled clumps that fell over her wrinkled face. Her bare
legs, in tattered cloth shoes as always, were pale white,
laced with blue veins. The southern sun had no effect on
Madame Stefano's skin.

Stefano himself was in charge of selling wine and liquor.
A robust and burly despot, Stefano, unlike his wife, did
not deprive himself of earthly pleasures. He loved to eat
well and drink a lot, and he loved women. He was a bully
and a troublemaker with whom people avoided conflict.
Between him and the other Neapolitans (most of the
town's inhabitants were from Naples, and only a few were

French), most of whom were related to him and were also named Stefano, existed an everlasting animosity. He kept away from them, as if he had been excommunicated.

Besides the flock of little children, the Stefanos had an older son, Joseph, a naval recruit in the nearby port, and a daughter, Jejette. An attractive peasant of sixteen with flushed gums and red eyelashes whose body was buxom and solid, she was good for any sort of work. She helped her parents in the store, worked in the kitchen and did all the housework, ran the café on the rooftop veranda, got drunk with her customers, danced the foxtrot and the waltz with them to the sounds of the hoarse gramophone, allowed her fleshy parts to be stealthily pinched, and laughed loud and often.

'Nice swimming, eh?' Stefano greeted them.

Gina wore only a skimpy bathrobe. The freshness of the water still clung to her face. Stefano set his eyes upon her feverishly. 'Hurry, Madame Stefano, I'm famished! Hey, you bastards! Look out for the wine!' Stefano roared across the street at the children crawling under a table set for lunch with a large bottle of wine, beneath the shade of a plane tree.

Madame Stefano and Jejette weighed the butter, cheese, fruits, and vegetables for Gina. Barth studied the tins of preserves stacked on the shelves.

'Do you have a child, madame?' Madame Stefano asked, her teeth shining.

'Not yet,' replied Gina.

'Hey! You haven't fulfilled your obligation,' Madame Stefano reproached Barth. 'A healthy woman like this, and pretty, too — you know you're pretty, madame!'

'And my husband?' asked Gina.

'Him, too, of course! I like him, ha-ha-ha!'

'You hear that?' said Barth to Stefano.

Stefano, who was bent over wine crates in the corner, rose to his formidable height. 'I agree, ha-ha-ha! My wife and Barth, and me and you, madame. A fair trade, isn't it?'

Jejette spread her lips in a conspiratorial smile.

'I'll think about it,' Barth said with forced humour.

Stefano raised a full bottle of rosé and waved it in the air. 'See this? You should get it. Try it and then come and tell me! I've never had rosé like this before.'

'Nice. We'll try it.'

'And some evening, why don't you stop by my café,' said Stefano as they were leaving. 'It's the world's meeting place! Come on over and we'll have a drink together.'

In the garden, Madame Bremon, beneath her wide straw hat, was scrubbing her laundry as usual in the trough by the well. Didi, her three-year-old grandson, tumbled on the ground with Bijou. Didi's head was large and round, set with bulging eyes. The torpid afternoon was embroidered with the droning hum of flies, Didi's muffled squealing, and the wet slapping of Madame Bremon's laundry. As Barth and Gina passed her, Madame Bremon told them that Cici, 'that Italian,' she added in a tone of dismissal (as masters of the land, the French here didn't like the Italians), had stopped by a few minutes ago to return a book that Gina had left on the beach.

Diligently Gina prepared dinner, Barth helping at her side. After a short while, they sat down in the dining room, which was shrouded in semi-darkness. Didi and Bijou gaped at them, their eyes eagerly following each movement, one with his thumb in his mouth, the other wagging his tail and blinking his bleary eyes.

'Here!' Gina offered them some bread with butter and cheese. Didi swallowed a sardine also, but Bijou turned it down.

The food and rosé left a pleasant weariness in their limbs. Soon after they finished, they retired to their room upstairs. There they remained, naked, two exquisite young bodies, saturated with sun and sea. An evil thought entered Gina's mind: how good it would be if gorgeous Marcelle were with them now, and maybe another beautiful woman, here, all together, in the rarefied dusk scented with perfume and cologne, and overflowing with the stunning vapours of lust ...

Who could have imagined the heart of man?

'Did you finish your soup, Didi?' Monsieur Larouette, Madame Bremon's son-in-law, would ask his son the same question every evening at exactly seven o'clock when he returned from Nice, where he worked as a bookkeeper for a wholesale oil-and-wine firm. Monsieur Larouette was short and broad-shouldered, his legs bowed in the shape of an urn. A straw cap was perched on the tip of his enormous skull. With a habitual motion, he tilted the cap back to his neck and wiped his face down from his forehead.

Madame Bremon poured him a glass of wine and offered him her usual answer regarding Didi: 'He ate well, and behaved as he should.'

Sitting on his father's lap, Didi nuzzled into him. Lifting his simple face, encrusted with sweat and dust, he pestered his father for a boat ride.

'Wait a while, Didi,' was the reply.

Monsieur Larouette's wife was staying a few weeks in the mountains because of an infected lung. But his mother, a fat, bilious matron, could be seen now, as on every evening at this time, spread out in an armchair by the door of her house, ten houses down the street. Her wicked face was pointed seawards, casting a pall of dread on Monsieur Larouette and Madame Bremon, her son's mother-in-law. She fabricated all kinds of ailments and considered herself dangerously ill. She had an extreme fear of walking, and was convinced that if she dared cross the street — even the twenty steps from her house to the beach — she would surely collapse and die. For this reason she wouldn't leave her doorstep, and sat with her body flowing over the edges of her chair, while she absorbed everything within earshot and acknowledged all the passers-by with responses according to their standing. She knew the gossip and slander of the town in all its detail, though no one knew where from, as she was never seen talking to anyone.

She controlled her house like a tyrant. No one would dare defy her word, or in any way disrupt the routine that she dictated. Her son, the sole heir to her worldly possessions, was forced to surrender his monthly earnings in full to her. She would issue him, as she would to a schoolboy, a few francs a week for his personal needs.

'Swimming in the sea is tiring, isn't it, madame!' Monsieur Larouette called through the open window to

Gina, who was sunk in a hammock on the small veranda. She swatted lazily at the hum of an invisible mosquito.

'The heat is oppressive. One must get used to it,' she replied.

'The heat doesn't bother me much.'

'Probably because you were born here.'

'True.' He emptied his glass of wine and stood up. 'Excuse me, but we must begin dinner. Come with me, Didi. Then your godmother will come for you.' Didi called Madame Bremon his godmother; he called only Madame Larouette his grandma. As he was leaving, Monsieur Larouette said, 'If you'd like, come for a short sail — after dinner.'

'Thanks. We'll see.'

'Better yet, on Sunday,' he added, 'then I'm free all afternoon.'

He left with Didi and Bijou, walking pigeon-toed.

When the day's heat had begun to subside, they stepped out of the house and, hesitating for a moment, looked back and forth along the street. Fishing boats were scattered across the sea as evening settled quietly upon them. The aroma of roasted fish arose from somewhere, and something at once strange and familiar saturated the air. Stefano sat outside with his family around the table, surrendering himself to a huge bowl of pasta and tomato sauce. He beckoned to Barth and Gina, but they declined his invitation and retreated to the opposite side of the street, passing the guesthouse, where guests were now sitting down in the garden for dinner. Among them were Latzi and Suzi, in high spirits as always, talking and laughing loudly. Slowly, they continued down the empty street, walking on dust that muffled their footsteps. They came to a villa hidden in a garden at the end of the street, from which burst the thick, slightly hoarse barks of an invisible dog. To their right, the sea had mingled with the evening, swallowing the fishermen and their boats. With the light, soothing spray underfoot, all at once one felt plucked from a place — somewhere indeterminate, but its shape was permanently imprinted in the soul, and one was re-attached to something else limitless that was both within and without. They stood for a short while in silence, filling their lungs with the freshness of the evening, before returning.

The spacious café near Madame Larouette's house was empty. A lonely light bulb shared its meagre light with a covered veranda.

'Hey, *patron!*' Barth shouted into the empty room. A dark-skinned young girl brought them cold lemonade.

Cici appeared immediately after, squat and square in his dark dress shirt, its collar thrown open. His palms were hard and flat as boards, his muscular arms round and thick like iron bars. His broad, prominent jaw testified to his athletic bearing. He sat opposite Gina.

'Aren't you back at work now?' Barth asked.

'My boss is in Normandy for a few weeks, so we have nothing to do until he returns.'

Cici had been living here for three years, engaging himself in all sorts of temporary work, as he had no specific skills. During the fishing season, when the schools

of sardines were sighted, he took to the sea with the fishermen in the evenings, remaining with them through the
night, spreading and hauling their nets. Lately, he worked
with the Arab as a builder. They were working on a three-
storey building behind Stefano's house, which was about
to be finished. They had done everything by themselves:
framing, flooring, and installing doors and windows. They
had turned a small ground-floor room into a bedroom,
with two old metal cots, and lived there as they worked, in
the midst of the pungent odours of cement, plaster, paint,
and sawdust.

Gina's blue cotton dress suited her. A red woollen shawl
was loosely draped over her shoulders. Her flushed face,
on which the sun's rays had cooled by now, resembled a
ripe, velvety fruit, and was wrapped in a relaxed expression. Cici sat across from her, unable to take his eyes off
her. A full glass of beer stood on the table before him, its
head of foam disappearing while he studied her. He rose
and went to switch on the gramophone. After wiping his
hands with a handkerchief, he bowed with exaggerated
politeness and asked Gina to dance to a sweet, raspy waltz.
He danced elegantly, pliant and graceful despite his short
stature, leading well. But his heavy hand scorched her back
like red-hot iron, and Gina was relieved when the waltz
was over. Cici wiped the sweat from his face.

'No,' Gina said, 'it's not easy dancing tonight. The heat
gets trapped in your limbs.'

Barth sat and smoked, relentlessly battling the mosquitoes, which bit through the cloth sandals on his feet. He
stood up and danced a charleston with Cici, the two of

them shaking their bodies towards each other and swaying from side to side like ships tossed on a stormy sea.

'So where is the boat you once mentioned?' Gina turned to Cici.

'It's Stefano's brother's boat. It has a leak.'

'Pity. On a night like this I would have loved to sail.'

'I'll try to find another. Maybe tomorrow, if Marco doesn't go fishing.'

'Bored?' said Barth. 'After the sun sets, the charm of a place like this changes. I can only imagine the winter, and the rainy days.' He suggested going to Stefano's. 'It's not as cramped, at least,' he said. At first Cici declined to join them. Several days before, he had had words with Stefano. But he reconsidered and accompanied them nonetheless.

Stefano's rooftop veranda was reached by a staircase built onto the outer wall of his house. The gramophone was already hoarse from blaring wild jazz. Latzi was dancing with Suzi. The Japanese fellow and his companion were drinking black coffee and cognac, while several villagers, young fishermen and their wives, were drinking red wine with Stefano. Jejette was serving the guests and tending to the gramophone, exposing her flushed gums and lips in constant laughter.

No sooner had they sat than the Japanese fellow asked Gina to dance. Cici followed their twirling with darkening eyes. In a single gulp, he emptied the glass of cognac that Jejette had brought. Gina returned, exhausted. She had had enough for one night. She couldn't dance anymore. Yet when Stefano approached, she gave in so as not to embarrass him, despite the disgust that his closeness aroused in her. Cici sat as though on glowing coals. As if to take revenge on somebody, he rose to dance, alternating partners: first Jejette; then the Englishwoman, the Japanese fellow's friend; then Suzi, who was a full head taller than he; and back again. But his mood remained foul.

Barth, who was smoking endlessly, his long legs crossed, chuckled to himself. The reason for Cici's sudden change of mood hadn't escaped his notice, and he saw it as slightly ridiculous. How could that Cici ever imagine this? Couldn't he understand that it could go nowhere? The vast gap between Gina and Cici, two beings so distant and different from each other, could never be bridged. Barth could rest assured: Cici was not the man to take Gina from him!

Marcelle appeared with a friend, a young Parisian girl, unattractive, who was staying awhile with her parents in their private villa. The two girls joined Gina and Barth at their table. Immediately Barth's bored expression disappeared from his face. 'The sea suits you, Mademoiselle Marcelle.'

'I love the sea, it's true.' And she added: 'I could bathe night and day.'

'Yet you don't bathe that often,' Gina remarked.

'The doctor forbade it. He even suggested I go to the mountains. But my aunt lives here.'

The moon had risen. A shimmering carpet of silver spread across the sea, towards the horizon. The waves glittered like sequins. From nowhere, a rich baritone voice swelled into a poignant Italian folk song. Gina half shut her eyes and leaned back against the railing of the veranda. The cigarette in her hand went out. But Stefano's coarse laugh, which burst from the neighbouring table at that moment, tore something just beginning to form inside her. She threw an angry glance up at him. As though reading her thoughts, Marcelle said, 'How crude he is!'

A dark tranquillity was spilling over the village and onto the sea. On this evening, in this place, one felt screened from despair. For no particular reason, Barth thought of the director of the office in which he worked as head engineer. An ageing bachelor sporting a pointed beard scattered with grey, he was a man free of all lusts and passions. His weekly day off was always one of mortification, since he had no idea what to do with it. And if sometimes by chance Barth stopped in at the office on a weekend afternoon to finish a sketch, the fellow would consider it a special kindness, for it would ease his tedium. Barth felt sorry for the old man, whose pointed beard now seemed quite pathetic to him, as if it itself expressed the banality and cheerlessness of the man's life. He looked at Marcelle — her narrow face, delicately outlined; her dark-grey eyes shaded by long lashes; her full mouth thirsting for life — and he could not understand how any man could feel miserable as long as such beautiful creatures were still to be found. And Gina herself! Wouldn't just a single glance from her suffice to dull the bitter stings that pierce a man? Indeed, he thought, fate had been good to him. It had afforded him a precious woman with whom to arrange his life as a summer scene, one in which even the thunderclouds offered a blessing. He picked up her hand to stroke it. Gina gave him a loving smile.

'You are staying here until autumn, I presume?' Barth turned to Marcelle.

'Until the end of August. What do you expect? One has to work.'

'To work? Your face belies it.'

'Even so, I am in nursing school.'

Stefano was dancing with Jejette now. Cici could not resist remarking that such a relationship between father and daughter wasn't normal, a fact known to all; yet nobody reported him.

'They're afraid of him. No one wants to put his life on the line.'

Afterwards, the interpreter arrived, accompanied by the Arab. They joined the other group — the Japanese fellow, Latzi, and their women. The interpreter immediately took off his jacket and began to dance with each woman in turn, his artificial hand resting limply on his partner's shoulder. His laugh was hollow and hoarse, without feeling. Marcelle said that she could not bear him, this interpreter, for there was something false in his nature. Cici came feebly to his defence, then stopped. After all, he had only met him here and had known him just a short time.

Barth looked out along the sleepy road, anointed with moonlight. Along the carpet of pebbles sloping to the sea, several fishing dories were scattered. Opposite some of them, drowsy fishermen gathered with their wives and children. They lived in the houses across the street and slept here in the coolness of the night. Small waves wandered from the horizon to stroke the shore with light, muffled slaps. The scene, rendered in the moon's gossamer light, seemed unreal.

'If only we could bathe now!'

Barth immediately caught on to the Parisian's idea. 'Why not? It's not cold at all. And you, Gina?'

'Don't be silly. It's not worth catching pneumonia.'

Marcelle was ready to join in. And Cici, whose good spirits had suddenly returned, felt as if he could stay in the water a half-hour or more, if they would.

Barth went in with Marcelle first. Behind them were Cici, Gina, and the Parisian girl. Barth put his arm through Marcelle's. 'Do you realise that you're beautiful?'

'So I've been told,' she said, turning with a smile.

Ah, this Marcelle certainly knew how to smile enchantingly. A pang of sorrow touched Barth's heart at the sight of her delicate, seductive smile. He was suddenly filled with a torrent of extra strength. Now would be the right time to run until breathless, to jump, to climb a tree, to be embroiled in combat. The warmth of her bare arm flowed through his shirtsleeve like a current of electricity. Yes, now he must plunge in; it was no longer a whim. The heat was overbearing on this cool and dewy night. As if to himself, he muttered, 'It's true. I haven't seen many women as beautiful as you, and I've had the occasion to see women, after all!'

'Your wife.'

'I could say this to her face. She is too beautiful to be jealous of a friend of hers.' Unintentionally he squeezed her arm. The pebbles crunched underfoot. 'Here we are!' He let go of her arm and turned around. 'Well, children!'

In vain Gina tried to dissuade them. Hidden behind a nearby boat, Cici and Barth stripped off their clothes, and in one leap threw themselves stark naked into the water. The girls followed. Barth caught a fleeting glimpse of Marcelle's nude body as she ran the few steps to the water.

'It's not cold at all!' he called to Gina, who sat close to the shore. He moved closer to Marcelle and swam beside her. He touched her by accident while swimming, and caught his breath. 'This swim. I'll never forget it,' he said, whispering so Cici wouldn't hear.

Marcelle burst into laughter for no reason.

'Come out,' Gina urged, 'you'll all catch cold and die!'

He could have swum all night, but in spite of that, he hurried out. He wiped the drops of water from his body, rubbed his skin vigorously, and began some strange callisthenics to increase his circulation, for it turned out that the air was cooler than the water. His movements seemed stranger still in the glow of moonlight.

'What's this for? Why?' Gina snapped as he, now dressed, approached her.

'We have to run!' Barth said as the others appeared. 'Let's go. To the guesthouse: we'll see who's first!'

Everyone ran, except Gina. Afterwards he stopped to wait for her.

The guesthouse was already dark. Empty tables and chairs could be seen through the fence in a patchwork of moonlight. A dog came running down the street, his paws sinking mutely in little clouds of dust. As he approached, it became clear that the dog was none other than Bijou, spotted black and white. He recognised Barth and lingered, turning his head towards the rest of the group opposite the guesthouse. Then he approached, wagging his tail and affectionately licking Barth's hand. Hoarse melodies continued to shower down from Stefano's roof across the street. Couples whirled, and a large pool of electric light washed from his roof almost to the edge of the sea.

'I'll go with you to Nice.'

'No, I'll be going alone.'

Cici's expression was imperious. His jaws tightened. 'Can you stop me from coming?'

'Of course not. But I do want to go alone.'

'If you only knew, madame.' He looked down and continued: 'I'm prepared, if you command, to cross the sea, to swim to Algiers, or to starve for two weeks.' He put the palm of his hand to his shirt, over his heart. Gina stifled her laugh. Cici looked up. 'I'd rather you didn't laugh.'

'Aha! You forbid me?'

'I'm from Naples, madame!' Cici tossed a pebble into the air. 'In Naples we behead people.'

'Ah.'

'We behead them,' repeated Cici.

'Great. So what?'

Cici was silent. Gina spread a towel over her thigh, which the sun had begun to redden. 'If you are a friend of Barth's, then why don't you talk like this when he's with us? Try and speak like this to his face.'

'I could say it to his face; I have nothing to hide.' He paused. 'You'd better not torture me.'

'You're talking nonsense, Monsieur Cici.'

'You are the only woman, the first. I haven't loved a woman like this yet.'

'How does this affect me? I can't imprison myself in a box. I have never encouraged you.'

'They say you aren't married to him at all.'

'So what! It's nobody's business.'

Cici lowered his head and bent down, mechanically sifting gravel through his fingers. Gina's face was flushed to the roots of her hair. She said, 'You're going too far, monsieur! If you want me to continue talking to you, you will have to stop speaking such nonsense.'

Cici didn't answer. He had gone too far. But what difference did it make? He was filled with a wretched sadness. Why had she come here, of all places, to spend her vacation? Weren't there enough beaches in the world? 'And so, you don't want me to join you?'

'No.' She turned over to her other side under the umbrella. 'When my husband gets well, you can join us sometime.'

'Since the day you arrived, I haven't been able to sleep. I've lost my appetite. When I see you, I feel like I'm going to burst.' And after a moment: 'An Italian doesn't talk like this for nothing. You'd better get out of this place while there's still time.'

'If you don't stop immediately, I'll ask you to leave.'

'Excuse me, madame.'

Nearby, Latzi and Suzi were romping on the beach with the interpreter and the Arab. The interpreter was somewhat tanned by now, though the difference between him and his friends was still immediately obvious. The remnant of his arm was wrapped in a towel as usual. Gina could overhear fragments of their conversation — about Italy and about Nice. She felt slightly intimidated by the man beside her, who belonged to another species, another social stratum, whose character was not clear enough to her. It was impossible to know what he was capable of. Nevertheless, she was unconsciously aroused by his unbridled passion. Gina had a coquettish side: in a hidden corner of her soul, it was somehow pleasurable to be the cause of a man's insomnia, a man who two weeks ago had not been aware of her existence.

Gina glanced at Cici. He sat dark and motionless. His collar was thrown open over his shoulders, revealing the broad curve of his bare chest. This strong man, resembling a cast bronze statue in his stance, seemed so pitiful seated next to her in his misery.

The water quietly washed the shore. Nearby crawled a boat filled with naked bodies, noise, and laughter. Stefano's brood, accompanied by Marcelle and her Parisian friend, were in it. Stray arms and legs, outstretched over the gunwales, splashed the water. The sounds of their voices were interspersed with a heavy, intense silence. A tall Englishman glided sidestroke along the shore, followed faithfully by his slender Great Dane. Twice a day, in the morning and early evening, the Englishman would swim the same distance with his dog, behind Stefano's house and along the length of the entire village — always in the same straight line, as if swimming in an invisible lane. For a while Gina followed them with her eyes.

The ice-cream peddler appeared on the street with his pushcart, announcing his wares in a husky voice. Gina rescued Cici from his ruminations by giving him some change to buy some ice cream. When he returned, he sat beside her again, folding his legs beneath him. He studied her avidly as she licked her cappuccino-coloured ice cream.

'Why didn't you buy one for yourself? Didn't I ask you to?'

Cici dismissed the question with a wave of his hand. 'You have a hard heart, madame.'

'You think so?'

After a minute, as he dug in his pack of cigarettes: 'Is it because I'm a labourer ...'

'You're talking nonsense! I love my husband.'

'I'm no more a fool than anyone. I haven't read books, but I've thought about what's on my mind.' He tapped his finger to his forehead.

'I don't doubt it. Give me a cigarette.'

Cici continued, 'I may go to Paris; I'll find a living there, too. I could sell fish. I have connections.'

Gina blew smoke rings, neatly formed in the sun. For a while she studied the nails on her outstretched toes, then turned her head back towards the nearby group, which by now included Marcelle. Marcelle waved to her, smiling warmly. In front of Stefano's store a truck was being unloaded of a barrel and several crates with black inscriptions. Stefano's awesome roar was heard. Madame Stefano appeared at the door in her bare white feet and unkempt hair.

'You're quiet, madame. You have nothing to say to me.'

'Nothing.'

'Tonight I'll get a boat —'

'Not tonight. When my husband gets better.'

'How you torture me.' He rose suddenly, as if he had reached an important decision, and walked to the water.

'I'm so glad you came.'

Barth lay in bed, wearing grey silk pyjamas, the sheet pulled up to his chin. The room was awash with a warm semi-darkness.

'One should visit the sick,' said Marcelle.

'I'm not seriously ill.' Barth laughed. 'If you hadn't come today — I'll surely get up tomorrow.'

'You've been here five days. What did you have then?'

'A fever. Slight congestion. Now it's all over.'

'It must mean that swimming at night is dangerous. It's a wonder I didn't fall ill too, since I'm very sensitive.'

'You see, sometimes it's those who aren't sensitive who're struck. Don't you want to move your chair a little closer, so I can see your face?'

'And where is Gina?'

'She's gone to Nice on some errand.'

Marcelle leaned back in her chair. A necklace of blue glass clung to her. The richness of her tan was emphasised by her white cotton dress. Her thighs, dusted with a light down, were shapely and muscular, like a dancer's.

Barth gazed at her quietly for a moment. Then he ran his fingers through his thick blond hair to the back of his neck. 'Your hat: don't you want to take it off?'

Marcelle did as he asked. She placed her broad white panama on a chair. With a graceful shake of her head, she fluffed her curly black hair, cut like a boy's. For some reason she smiled an absent smile to herself. 'It's so warm in here, warmer than outside.'

Barth sat up and took Marcelle's hand, long and slender, and touched it to his lips. He held it close, stroking it tenderly many times.

The house was imbued with a deep stillness. The buzz of a hidden fly, just awakened, enriched the yearning silence and became part of it. Soon it was broken by the burst of a child's cry outside. The voice sounded like Didi's, and Barth imagined his plump face, contorted by tears and turning ugly, as he had seen it many times.

Her head tilted slightly, Marcelle sat slumped, close to the bed, her magnificent eyes gazing straight ahead. She was listening to an enchanted world that existed all at once and not at all, one hand absently stroking the sculpted arm of the chair, the other surrendered to Barth. After a moment, she pulled her hands back and crossed her legs.

'So tomorrow you'll already be getting up?'

'Tomorrow I'll be getting up …' After a moment, he murmured, as if to himself: 'It was clear to me all along that you would come. I've been waiting all along. Whenever footsteps scratched in the garden, my whole self sprang up towards you. And I —' He stopped mid-sentence and fixed his eyes on her.

Marcelle remained seated, leaning back, her head turned slightly from him, a warm smile cast upon it. Her eyes were half closed, hidden through long lashes.

Between her slightly parted lips, smooth and even teeth shone white, seeming whiter still against her bronze skin and the hint of down at the corners of her mouth, which lent an indescribable beauty to her features.

There she was, sitting in front of him, Marcelle. The nymph as distant from his life as the limits of the earth, yet within the reach of a hand. And at that moment it became clear to him that a man was able to extract in a single instant the essence of all the joy allotted him for a lifetime, and to feed on it for the rest of his days, from that moment alone. All the fatigue remaining in Barth from the fever melted away.

Outside, the husky voice of the ice-cream peddler could be heard as if from another world. He called out in monosyllabic cries. A molten silence stretched between each cry. Barth turned his body towards Marcelle, until his head almost touched hers. He peered deeply into her delicate eyes for a few minutes, his heart exploding with each pulse. All of a sudden, he wrapped his arms around her neck and pulled her towards him. Darkness settled upon the world, past, present, future. Their lips mingled with each other's.

Then she freed herself from his arms. On either side of her nose a slight pallor rose. Unable to control his hands, Barth peeled off her dress, and the slip beneath it. She let loose a muffled laugh, slightly hoarse, and jumped onto Barth's bed, sinking her teeth into his neck, his shoulders and chest, like a wildly stampeding animal.

Gina planned to return on the six o'clock train. She had stayed on for two hours to stroll at her leisure and look at the lovely things in the shop windows. She stood erect, her lightly tanned face revealing an inner fire despite her tranquil expression. Her silk dress was the colour of wild strawberries, and there were large hoops in her ears. She exuded the fragrance of exotic countries, from lands across the ocean where people ran naked, their impulses wild and noble, rooted in prehistoric times and God. Men stopped in their paths, wondering about the arrogance of her stance, or the splendour of her movements. Some turned and followed her and tried with jumbled half-sentences to coax her into a café or a casino. The heat bore the choking scents of the city. The horses' heads were dressed in tattered straw hats, dusty with age. Their ears poked through two holes and twitched incessantly against the biting flies.

As she turned onto the main boulevard, Cici appeared before her, dressed in his best Sunday suit.

'Oh?' Gina was taken aback.

'I don't mean to trouble you, madame. I'll go away, if that's what you want.' Squat, square, and muscular as a lumberjack, he stood before her. His bare head rested on his shoulders without the grace of a neck.

The words slipped from Gina's mouth, in spite of herself: 'You can walk with me awhile.' And within a minute she corrected herself: 'A half-hour at most, then you must leave me.'

Cici's face lit up. He made a motion to kiss her hand, but she pulled back, with a gesture of disgust unnoticed by him.

Amid the bustle of the boulevard he strode beside her, so small and pathetic in comparison to her. For a while he was silent. Yet a great exhilaration pounded within him, his pulse exulting for the magnificent woman beside him. He cast his gaze directly ahead, without seeing anything. 'Lately I've been working from the inside scaffolding. I also had work to do outside, in the shade. All the same, I worked all day long in the sun, because from there I could see you walking to Stefano's store and to the beach.'

Gina pretended not to hear. The heat was wrapped around her like a bandage. The wide boulevard seemed too narrow for her. And the squat Italian who clung to her, with his face red as brick, couldn't ease the heat; quite the contrary. 'I thought you were going to visit my husband.'

'I couldn't stay back there. I just wanted to hear you say that you didn't hold it against me.'

'No, why should I?'

'I think I didn't behave politely this morning.'

Gina stopped from time to time at the shop windows. She entered a cosmetics store to buy something. Cici waited outside for her. They continued along the boulevard that led to the beach, the casino, the big hotels, and the mansions that stood facing the sun and the sea. The shore here was very colourful with the beach umbrellas, the tents, and the bathing suits of the many bathers. Along the sparkling asphalt of the beach road, cars flew back and forth, honking noisily. The casino's veranda was filled to capacity, and the band was tuning up for the afternoon's dance.

No, Gina did not accept Cici's invitation to the casino.

She reminded him that his time was up and that he had to leave her. Cici obeyed, and walked in the opposite direction. Yet a few minutes later, she saw him, not far away, leaning against the pier, facing her. Furious, she stopped a taxi and jumped in. She let herself out in the centre of the city, where she sat down at a sidewalk café, and breathed deeply, as if redeemed.

When she had finished her iced coffee, she put on some lipstick and lit a cigarette. *What an annoyance! Let him find me now!* But she was struck by a wave of pity for this man, and had he appeared now and sat beside her, she certainly would not have protested.

She leaned back, enjoying her respite from the bustle of the street. As she studied the passers-by, examining the faces and dresses of the women, it got hotter and hotter. The pulse of life was pounding forcefully, as strong within her as without. Aware of her physical sensations, she was aroused with love for her mysterious and agitated body, as if, somehow, it were a creation apart from her.

A man seated at the next table, who hadn't taken his eyes off Gina all this time, slid his chair over. As if continuing a conversation interrupted only a minute ago, he said: 'This city must be seen in the spring. It is lovely then.'

He was a man of about thirty, his face open and his gaze direct, inspiring trust.

Gina smiled. 'Who would you have said that to if I had not entered this place?'

'I wouldn't have said it.'

'But now you feel like praising the city.'

'Hmmm … not exactly.' He called the waiter to bring

him a pack of cigarettes. 'Actually, I'd like to offer you my sincerest thanks.'

Gina raised her eyes to him, surprised.

'Because you came here and you are so beautiful.'

'I have to admit, I hadn't thought of coming here to give you pleasure.' She smiled again.

'It's all the same.' He opened the pack of cigarettes and pushed a finger inside. He wiped his broad, handsome forehead. 'You see, madame, sometimes a person wakes up in the morning, and everything is as it should be. The summer presents itself to him. The sun has painted a bit of a window at the top of the blue wall. The bustle of the street has the same smell and colour as the day before. Apparently, nothing has changed, not even a bit, isn't it so? And yet he immediately feels that this is not it. Something is missing today. Suddenly he can't understand the meaning of the simplest things, neither their relationship to himself nor their relationship to one another — as if it became clear that the ultimate purpose, that which gives value to every thing and deed, is not there at all ... Then he continues, out of habit, with his daily trivial actions — everything is fine. Except that from that point on there is no meaning to it all.'

He lit the cigarette, which had gone out.

'And suddenly, quite by chance, there appears a strange woman, and all at once he is reconnected to the world.'

After a short silence, he said, 'If I'm not mistaken, madame is from Germany.'

'Let's say from Vienna.'

'Well then, we can rid ourselves of the constraints of a foreign language.'

But Gina was preparing to leave, lest she miss her train.

'Wait, why? You'd do me an honour by letting me drive you. In ten minutes you'll be home.' He introduced himself as Irwin Kraft from Munich, a prosecuting attorney who had retired because to make a profession of revealing other people's crimes was against his nature.

At that moment, Cici passed hastily in front of the café, on his way to the nearby station. Gina smiled gleefully to herself as she imagined his disappointment at not finding her there.

'And so you float around at leisure in your car?'

'Something like that.'

'Not a bad life.'

'Not always.'

He suggested a drive through the city before taking Gina to her destination. Gina sat beside him in the large grey sedan. They meandered through the network of streets, some of which rose steeply up the hills on which the city rested. They passed through the quarter where villas hid in tranquil gardens, and continued along the cobalt bay, which looked like a picture on a postcard. A refreshing wind blew towards them. And when he let her off by Madame Bremon's house, they agreed that he would return one day soon, to take them for a trip.

The interpreter was trilling Italian folk songs in a shrill voice, while the Arab sat beside him, smoking. In spite of the door to the balcony being open, the room was filled with an asphyxiating heat.

The table, usually extended, had been pushed next to

the sofa in order to make room for guests. Many bottles had already been emptied, and limbs were already leaden. Latzi wanted to dance, just to dance; and the Japanese fellow, who was hosting the party, took care of that as well. The gramophone and a stack of records stood ready on a stool in the corner.

Suzi chatted with Gina, and then seated herself beside Barth.

'You're not drinking, Monsieur Barth. Apparently you prefer to be the only sober one among drunkards, to see them in their foolishness.'

'Not so. I've drunk more than anyone. What can I do if drink has no effect on me! Anyway, the night is young.'

The Japanese fellow's companion sat close to them on the sofa. She fanned her hot, leathery face with a colourful paper fan. She refilled Barth's glass and handed it to him. 'Then you can drink to the health of all the beautiful women here!'

Barth did as she asked. 'Cheers to the mistress of the house especially, and to all beautiful women in general!'

The flesh along this small woman's neck was wilted, scattered with many fine pendulous wrinkles, hanging limp like an empty sack. The burden of all her years was borne by this neck. Yet Suzi was brimming with rude health and joyous vitality, though somehow dull.

'Will you be coming to Vienna soon?' she asked Barth.

'Perhaps in the winter. For Christmas.'

'Then you must visit us! Call first, or just pop in to the Café Museum. We're there every evening.'

'Great. I'll remember that.'

Latzi had switched on the gramophone and was dancing with Marcelle. Cici invited Gina to dance and, in the middle of it, blurted in her ear: 'That strange man interests you more than I do.'

'Which strange man?'

'The one who brought you back from Nice in his car three days ago.' Cici was already a little drunk; his tongue was looser.

'Listen, mister!' exclaimed Gina. 'Who gave you permission to spy on me?'

'I wasn't spying. I just happened to see.'

'I forbid you to follow me! Do you hear?'

'I won't tell anyone. Don't worry. I also saw you sitting with him in the Café Monaco.'

'Don't speak to me anymore!' Her voice quivered with rage.

At that moment, the waltz finished, and she went to sit beside Marcelle. Cici gulped down a glass of wine. His jaws were loosening even more. Now that the gramophone was silent, the interpreter started singing again. And Cici was humming along, his untrained voice deep and turbid. The waves of the warm melody spilled over the balcony into the darkness of the night, which was furrowed with light breezes like a man's breath, and into the breadth of the sleepy sea. A hidden tremor stirred in the hearts of the listeners, and a strange, burning day shimmered before them, spread over fields of yellow grain on the plains of a nostalgic land. Then Latzi, accompanied by his wife, sang a Viennese folk song:

Ja, ja, der Wein is' gu—et,
I' brauch' kei' neuen Hu—et.
I' setz' mei' alten auf,
Bevor i' a Wasser sauf'.[*]

Gina leaned against the balcony railing. She looked at the deserted midnight street and beyond, towards the sea that heaved silently, interwoven with the night into one great weight. A slight sadness rose within her, but it was not entirely unpleasant. For some reason, she recalled a night, a few years ago, when she had first come to know Barth. After a long walk in the Prater parks, she had stood in her room before an open window, also facing the summer night, and the fondness of her feelings towards Barth, as if swelling from that night into her soul, filled it to overflowing and compelled her to cry and sing. Through a dense silence, she had seemed to sense the strike of a match, an imaginary scratch in the next room, where her father might have lit a cigarette while studying his textbooks. Her father, Prof. Karl Funken: his eyes were filled with supreme wisdom and understanding, and could probe the depths of her soul so painlessly, those eyes that she loved. He was a rare person, whose presence alone could soothe the heart with comfort and strength. Actually, she had been lucky, Gina thought. Her life had flowed with pleasure, full and clear, without the superfluous turbulence that might disrupt her balance.

---

[*] German: 'Yes, yes, the wine is good / I don't need a new hat / I'll put my old one on / Before I drink some water.'

Her love for Barth, deep, consistent, never knowing fatigue or boredom, contributed a lot to it.

Latzi drew closer, quietly, and uprooted her from her thoughts. 'Excuse me, madame, if I'm interrupting; for some time I have wanted — I mean your face is very interesting. One could make an excellent portrait. I would very much love to paint your portrait.'

This man bothered her. A real barber, she thought, as she dismissed him with a monosyllabic answer and hurried inside. She sat in an empty chair beside Barth, who was talking to Marcelle and didn't notice her coming. A line that slipped out of his mouth that very minute made her somehow shiver. 'The way something appears is sometimes different from the way it is; it could even be its opposite ...' Gina wondered about the nagging feeling that this line, which apparently did not refer to her, inspired in her. Moreover, she felt an inexplicable fear of continuing their conversation, as if something that would truly sadden her might be said along the way. She felt compelled to end it immediately. She moved her chair nearer Barth and put her hand on his arm. He turned to her and smiled softly.

'What is it, Gin?' he whispered enticingly, and added, 'Are you bored?'

Gina gazed at him, her dark eyes now tinged with the light sadness that was so familiar to him. He stroked the skin of her cool arm, smooth like the skin of a peach, until her face lightened into a scant smile. 'People aren't happy here,' she said, 'or maybe it just seems that way to me.'

Facing them with his back to the wall, Cici looked at

her, his heavy, insistent gaze not leaving her for a moment. It made her uncomfortable. 'Maybe it would be best if we went to sleep.'

'Soon,' replied Barth without moving.

The gramophone began to play again. Gina rose, pulling Marcelle with her to dance. In a corner of the room, the Japanese fellow, tipsy by now, kept kissing Jacqueline, the little Parisian, Marcelle's friend, who from time to time uttered a sharp, grating laugh. Not far away sat the Englishwoman, a foolish smile settling on her flushed face. Through the mists of foxtrot and alcohol, she gestured to them with her fan. The interpreter pulled her from her stupor and began to dance with her.

They went out onto the drowsy road — Gina, Barth, and Marcelle. They walked quietly in the middle of the dewy street, and the tepid night slowly lifted the alcoholic haze from them. The mixture of drunken voices and the sounds of the gramophone receded into the background, becoming weaker and weaker, until it ceased to exist. A remnant of the evening's vapid feeling remained inside Gina. She felt empty and bored. A warm fatigue was spreading through her limbs. She sat on one of the rocks that were scattered along the length of the beach.

'Eating and drinking, that's an intimate matter. There is something immodest in doing so with strange people to whom you have no tie.'

'Sometimes one forms a connection by sharing a meal,' Barth remarked.

Sitting with their backs to the sea, they looked at the

row of darkened houses and were filled with the night's loneliness. Far away, a few short barks punctured the night as if with nails. Then nothing else. Just behind them, the ocean heaved ceaselessly with muffled breath.

After a moment, they rose and continued their walk to the edge of the village, to the point where the shore outlined a semicircle, as if embracing the water. They then retraced their steps, and turned into the side street where Marcelle lived. When Gina and Barth returned to the main road, Cici caught up with them. He was running towards them, extremely upset, almost crying. It was a bizarre sight. He began to talk immediately, in fragments, and in a choked voice quite unlike him.

'You understand, and madame will excuse me … such a disgrace! Don't think I'm drunk … I'm not drunk, not a bit, you hear! … I'm not trying to defend myself — it's not my nature … you know me a little! I don't want to embellish anything … Imagine, a man drunk as Lot, as a skunk, who can't tell a cow from a chicken! So what did he do to me, you ask? Nothing … absolutely nothing. I asked forgiveness from him, I cried in front of him, I kissed him … I am a man of justice, you can tell! That's my nature! … and he forgave me … in front of everyone he forgave me, and cried too … But I'm not sure if he did it for show and because he was drunk. He was the only one who was really drunk, much more than the interpreter or Latzi. But how can I be sure? I don't want him to hold a grudge … because I admit my mistake soberly and I regret it, you're my witnesses. Everyone cried with us and everyone kissed everyone else … but …'

'But what happened there?' Barth interrupted. 'Tell things the way they were!'

'Tell … there's nothing to tell … It's not even interesting … Do you find a smack interesting? This work, I don't like it … better call it an accident, an idiotic incident, than a premeditated act. It just happened, and only then did I realise it. But drunk I am not … He was drunk, not me.'

They were passing by the Japanese man's house, from which burst a thunderous hail of wild laughter. Cici stopped, and stretched his arm out towards the orange squares of light of the door and the two open windows: 'Here, can you hear? They're laughing! … Laughing! Unless they're hiding their grudge under the laughter … the Japanese guy especially … him more than anyone else …'

'My God! Just tell us what happened!' Gina cried, excited.

'This is it, madame! Nothing happened, almost nothing … It's just that Jacqueline threw off her dress and danced naked. Suzi also stripped and danced. Then the Englishwoman joined them. Three of them naked. Because the three of them were drunk, and all danced. There is nothing to say against that. They were drinking and dancing, off and on. Afterwards, Jacqueline found herself in my lap, didn't she? Because the lights were back on … she was crying because she was drunk. I felt sorry for her. And so she sat on my lap and cried. And then the Japanese guy, naked also except for his bathing trunks, told me to get her off my lap, didn't he? Nothing wrong with that. Didn't he buy her with his own money? But the girl didn't feel like it. Because she said, "Watch out for Cici!

He knows how to box!" And the Japanese guy said to me, because he was drunk: "Really? You know how to fight? Let's see!" And he grabbed me by the nose and pulled me here and there like this —' Cici imitated the Japanese man's action with his own hand. 'You understand that it was not the pain but the humiliation. No one has ever dared pull me around by my nose. Everyone laughed at me. And then I jumped and planted a punch right under his eye. One of my best! ... His eye was totally swollen. And immediately I felt badly and asked forgiveness. With tears and kisses. Because maybe he had no bad intention — drunk as he was. And yet I was not drunk.'

Gina suddenly burst out laughing. By now they had reached their apartment and the garden gate, and Bijou pushed himself under the latch and threw himself on them with contented grunts. Barth shook him off with a slight rebuke.

'You're laughing, madame! There's no place for laughter here. Cici, his head is still in its place. You'd better not laugh! What do you say, Monsieur Barth? Did I act improperly? I'm neither a doctor nor an engineer, it's true, but I'm not a boor! And certainly not a villain, that's for sure! It's not my way to hurt anyone by word or by gesture, you'll admit that yourselves; the Japanese guy is a decent fellow, a drunk though. I regret the incident. I don't want him to hold a grudge. That's it. But there's no place for laughing here.'

'And you haven't drunk a thing all evening?' teased Gina.

'What do you mean, haven't drunk? I did drink. But

not much. Anyway, here, we're used to drinking. Have I ever acted like a drunkard? Here ... would you like to go for a sail now? I can take Marco's boat. No? Not because I insulted you, God forbid. If I insulted you unintentionally with anything I said, let me apologise.' He put his hand on his breast. 'Well, I should go back to the Japanese fellow right now.'

'Why don't you go to sleep?' said Barth. 'It's already three in the morning.'

'No, I wouldn't be able to sleep, not until I knew for sure that he has nothing against me.' Cici ran back to the Japanese man.

They were still in the middle of breakfast. Kraft, self-assured, greeted them simply. Although he had already eaten at his hotel, he agreed to drink a cup of coffee with them, 'out of friendliness'. A simple, modest goodness prevailed in Madame Bremon's dining room. The thin semi-darkness was sweetened by a spray of sunlight streaming diagonally through the door, in which joyous flies bathed.

Gina placed in front of him a saucer of jam, and buttered him a roll. Her being radiated a virginal freshness, yet something in her graceful movements, soft and animated, was imbued with motherly calm. Irwin Kraft, enchanted by her at first sight in a way not diminished by habit, felt a moment's secret sadness when he recalled another young woman whose essence had been quite different. The other would evoke feelings of confusion around her. Her movements, incoherent because of an inner disorder, always caused anxiety in people and in things, to a point where their unique identities were lost. In his imagination there flashed the image of a grotesque illustration of this idea: an upside-down table, its legs in the air, a change making it so ridiculous that now one didn't know for what use it was intended.

He leaned back in his chair and wiped his sticky mouth with a napkin.

'And now, I think — a pity to waste anything of such a beautiful day.'

Gina asked him to wait a moment for Marcelle. He must forgive her for inviting Marcelle to join them: she was a charming girl and wouldn't 'spoil the view'. She herself would run upstairs in the meantime to get ready.

Marcelle brought with her the radiance of the morning, burnished orange and blue. She sat diagonally across from Kraft, wearing a tight, steel-coloured dress and a similarly coloured beret. Light conversation flowed slowly, brightened by streaks of her clear laughter. Barth mused, with no bearing on the conversation, that this Kraft was actually endowed with something straightforward and captivating. How sharp Gina's perceptions were, how right and to the point her judgement of character! For this, one could rely on her, without a doubt or any hesitation.

Gina returned and everyone got to their feet. Within a few minutes, the car was rolling along the smooth road, glossy black, that ran like a spine through all the coastal villages, inlaid with the lush greenery of southern flora. Their first stop after a short drive was in a small bathing resort that had only recently become popular. It rose in the sun's heat with its new hotels the colour of chocolate, lemon, and light coffee; the casino adorned with miniature palms; the huge garages; the magnificent restaurants and their verandas shaded from the sun by huge, colourful umbrellas. It was an international meeting place for celebrities — sports heroes, beauty queens, film stars, polished salon writers, various adventure seekers, and simply crazy American women and their ilk, all wandering on the clean streets that spread out to the shore, half naked in their bathing suits and also in their pyjamas. Someone dressed in regular clothes would certainly seem of a different species.

Kraft parked the car by a pine grove set on top of a small hill next to the casino. They left their clothes in the car and walked through a small grove, where some bathers were sprawled on benches scattered among the trees or on the dark ground, which was covered with dry and trampled needles in a patchwork of glowing sunlight. Here and there a joyous laugh would sparkle in the viscous heat and reverberate through the silence of the tall trees. Freeing themselves of clothes renewed an innate sense of freedom. The touch of sunlight made their laughter clearer, somehow more wild and free. Although strangers to one another, they saw themselves as a single family: their nakedness cancelled the distance between them, making them fundamentally equal, as at the time of birth and death.

'I'm surprised you didn't decide to settle here,' said Gina, turning to Kraft. 'In the summer it's as if Nice were a hall decked for a party to which the guests didn't show up.'

'I prefer it to this pandemonium. Would you like to live here?'

'My drowsy fishing village? I wouldn't exchange it for anything.'

On the other side of the grove, which came suddenly to a steep slope, a swirling mélange of colours shone before them, sparkling in the sun: bathing paraphernalia and hundreds of boats gliding back and forth not far from the shore — a mixture of all the tones of the spectrum set against the sea's vivid blue, which softened as it approached the horizon, blending into the lighter pastel of the sky and fusing with the lush green groves and gardens to the right.

'Hey, boys! Who's ready to jump in?' Marcelle's good spirits imparted a beautiful lustre to her dark, half-laughing eyes, and animated her shapely limbs. She hopped from one foot to the other.

'I'm with you!' cried Barth.

'And you, Gina?'

'No.' She smiled. They were settled people, she and Kraft. Wasn't it so?

They descended the broad stairs that led from the grove to the water. Marcelle and Barth went down onto a narrow, damp wooden pier that ran from the shore to a point where the sea was deeper than a man's height and ended in a high, square platform with a board on one of its sides, inclined into the water for sliding. They swam far out to a chain of red buoys that enclosed an area reserved for swimming. Side by side on their backs, they gazed up into the depths of the sky, spilling still and pure upon them. The noise around them, pierced by shrieks, was slightly muffled, as though filtered through a curtain. At times they encountered an icy current, as if they had entered a root cellar. The violent change in temperature sent a shudder through their flesh, a shudder of panic. Immediately, a thought forced itself on him, the frightful possibility of a heart attack, although his heart was completely healthy. The newspaper would carry a typically terse announcement, the sort that the eye glances over inadvertently while one sips the morning coffee. At times like these, Barth would decide that if he ever made it out of the water, he would never swim again. Yet the next time, as soon as he touched the water, he was compelled to outdistance himself, as if driven by a youthful recklessness whose absurdity was not unknown to him.

'We're going back!' announced Barth, frightened, although he wasn't particularly tired.

In the midst of the great clamour, Gina and Kraft sat on the warm sand and waited for them, their feet outstretched to the little waves that broke on them. They walked into the water to rinse the sand from themselves as everyone returned to dress, for it was already noon.

Soon after lunch, they found themselves rolling down the lustrous road. The sea was to their left, now seen, now hidden, and its sight alone somehow sweetened the insufferable heat. The car sliced through the sleepy yellow air, drawing forth little tongues of wind that licked their faces and hair. How pleasant to cut through the flesh of the day, to wrest from it even the faintest comfort.

Sunk in the luxurious softness of the seat, Gina closed her eyes and imagined flying backwards, but then forced herself to gather her senses and re-align her sense of direction. But as she opened her eyes, she was seized for a moment by a slight dizziness. It became evident that despite her effort to orient herself in the direction she was going, she nevertheless experienced some confusion; and in that sudden shift to reality, it was as if something in her were jolted out of place. She repeated this game a few times. Then she fixed her gaze on Marcelle, who sat beside her. She focused on her profile, a silhouette of pure and open lines. A moment passed as the lines blurred and quivered before her eyes. From the imbroglio of vague sensations that stirred within her, one clear thought slowly detached itself and floated to consciousness. It was of prophetic certainty that needed no evidence: that no great evil would come to her from Marcelle, not now, not ever. For this, Gina stirred with sympathy for her, perhaps because for a moment she saw Marcelle as weaker than herself and unlikely to harm her in any way. She took her hand. Marcelle turned, looking at Gina strangely, as if shaken from a dream.

'Do you like him?' She gestured with her chin towards Kraft's back.

Marcelle considered the broad, straight back in the tight robe that revealed the agility and strength of an athletic man. 'He's not unpleasant.'

Without pause, Gina whispered, 'If you love him, jealousy is not in my nature …'

'Him?'

'Of course not.'

She started speaking about Barth — who was sitting with Kraft in the front seat — analysing his qualities and revealing his strengths before this Marcelle, as if driven by an impulse to heighten any danger.

'He's worthy of love,' she concluded. 'A woman who isn't carried away by him doesn't have her senses in the right place. That's my frank opinion.'

'Not a bad advertisement,' joked Marcelle. And then: 'Don't you think that all this would make you suspicious of him? Or are you prepared for it?'

'You've had the chance to get to know him a bit by now.' The car was crossing a bridge that spanned a broad, shallow river. Through its crystalline waters the rocks could be seen scattered along the bottom. Kraft turned to the back seat to announce that they were off to the mountains, not to visit tourist attractions but to go wherever the road led them.

At about four o'clock, Kraft stopped in front of an inn in a quiet mountain village whose streets were empty. Dogs dozed in the shade cast by the low houses, their trembling tongues wagging from side to side. They drank some bad coffee and had a light snack. The innkeeper, in his shirtsleeves, was armed with a sharply pointed moustache and a curl on his chin, on which remained a single long strand of beard, for vanity, perhaps. A spotted cat, basking in the peaceful day, sprawled across one of the solid brown tables.

'It seems as if the world is purged of all annoyance and noise. Suddenly you can hear the sound of your own voice, without a filter,' Barth said as he put a roll with butter, tomato, and cheese into his mouth.

'Not every man wants to hear himself,' Kraft pointed

out. 'Most run to the clamour.'

After a while they returned to the car and rolled up and down, stopping in one village and then in another, and when evening fell, they turned home, filled with the lowing of strange animals and intoxicated by the smells of a simple, innocent existence, old as the earth and ceaselessly regenerating for infinity.

The jukebox spilled muffled jazz into the darkened hall. A few couples twirled around casually. A red petrol pump stood tall in front of the café, which opened onto the highway. Cars flew past intermittently, their headlights blinding. From the nearby railroad station, behind the gardens that spread from the street, there rolled from time to time the clear, rhythmic sound of signal whistles, soon after which a train, heaving and huffing, would send a shriek into the hush of night.

They sat in the back garden, which bordered the long hall used for dancing. Moths and mosquitoes hovered around the bare light bulbs that hung between the eucalyptus branches. Red-and-white checked tablecloths covered the big round liquor tables.

Cici rose and entered the hall to feed the jukebox a fifty-centime piece. He returned to his place to the accompaniment of a husky, lazy waltz. He wanted to dance again. Gina declined on the pretext of fatigue. She drank the remainder of her liquor and continued to draw at her cigarette with short puffs.

'Is Monsieur Barth coming here to meet you?'

'We didn't plan on it.'

'And you didn't visit her?'

'Yes. This evening.'

'Her sickness isn't critical, I hope.'

'It's hard to say. Spitting blood. But she is better. Her fever is down.'

'Too bad. Such a charming girl. She doesn't look after herself. Swimming in the sea certainly doesn't help.'

'It seems so. She'll have to stay away from a few things. Her lungs can't bear such abuse.'

'But then … on your trip with the German, she was all right then.'

'She didn't fall ill until six days ago.'

'The beach isn't the same without her. She brought a carefree and playful spirit.' After a moment, he continued in a voice trembling with a touch of sadness not befitting his athletic bearing: 'The summer, you know, I look forward to it eagerly. Sometimes a visitor you may like happens to drop in.'

'A female visitor, you mean?'

'No, even a male. Simple enough. Winter is terribly boring here. As soon as I finish work I change my clothes and go to Nice. Almost every evening. To play cards and drink Pernod, I don't care.' He smiled at the third table, with a group of two men and three women, beside which an enormously heavy dog, spotted white and orange, panted.

'Sunday,' Cici lowered his voice, 'I was with them at Bouche-de-Loup. They needed a third, for the governess. After all, they have to keep her busy while they fuss with their own men. The tall one, see, the fat one, she's the mother. A widow. Worse than the daughter. The young one's husband works in Nice. He only comes every few days, appears in the evening, and is gone by morning. And here the merrymaking continues. After all, they're not ugly, neither the first nor the second. And the men are brothers, partners to a mother and daughter. Sometimes their father joins them.'

'They can often be seen at the beach, with a boy of about four.'

'The boy sleeps, as children do. And they make love.'

'And you took the nanny yourself.'

'She's no less than they, is she? Neither less pretty nor less young. Anyway, it was only during that trip. What can I say? A man gets bored, and feels sorry for someone, too.' He continued, 'Do you think I couldn't have had them, too? Anyone I want! But this one's more appealing to me. Her position doesn't affect me either way. By the way, I was invited to their house for dinner, but I didn't go.'

Gina eyed the third table from time to time, her curious but uninterested glance going from one face to another in the group, portions of whose loud conversation reached her. She was extremely bored. Several times this evening she had asked herself what demon had made her agree to join him at the café. She ordered another drink and emptied the glass in a single gulp.

'Are you planning to leave already?' cried Cici when he saw her reach for her handbag.

'We can still walk for a while,' she said without thinking, and regretted it at once.

Cici wouldn't let her pay. She would offend him by

doing so. It was customary for the gentlemen to pay, not the ladies. Furthermore, it was he who had invited her. She had to accede to his will; it seemed of such importance to him. His face was already flushed with the sense of injustice.

He suggested a different route, partly on the main road but mostly through garden paths. The evening percolated through a person, like a light and aromatic beverage. The lungs expanded. The half-moon appeared and disappeared periodically behind the bank of trees to their right, sometimes hanging motionlessly for a moment from an upper branch, casting its cool, peaceful light on the empty street glowing subdued, and on the gardens and vineyards that spread out to their left. There were no houses here, or they were hidden in deep gardens, invisible and far removed from the street. And from there, from the depths of the garden, an angry bark would burst occasionally, in response to their muffled footsteps. Treading casually, silently, sometimes together, sometimes apart, each was given to his own thoughts. The spaces between passing cars lengthened. There were no passers-by.

They turned onto the path, dark and narrow, the hedges on each side scratching their legs. Cici put his arm through hers. A slight tremor passed through her at the touch of his arm, but she let him do it. They continued in silence. Only Cici's breath could be heard, heavy and urgent. Gina was uncomfortable. His visible excitement, which spread to her, started little by little to conquer her being. What was happening to her? A strange languor had come over her limbs; paralysis. Walking became difficult for her. An animal stupor coated her insides and cast a fog upon her mind like the numbness following a strong drink. The pressure of a muscular arm was vaguely felt, as though far from the limits of her existence. She saw, and didn't see, the winding path strewn with rocks. She was walking like a sleepwalker.

They reached a small clearing. The narrow stream nearby sent its timid rush into the stillness. Mingled with the fragile rush of the stream, the fragrant night, and even the strange man, a feeling came upon her that she had always walked this path, and would continue along it until the end of her days. It was as if all her past life and the possibility for future life had been pumped out of her.

Blindly, she sank to the slope of the riverbank, with Cici outstretched at her feet, whispering incoherent words with scorching breath. No, Gina didn't understand a thing. She only sensed her body burning, as if touched by fever. And Cici's scalding, biting kisses on her hands, on her bare arms, on her neck, on her face. In these kisses was the stomping of a mad, murderous animal. Had she wanted to protest, she would not have been able. And had he wanted to kill her, she would not have protested. She had no control of herself whatsoever. Indistinctly, she felt something happening in her body, something that was terrible and caused a deadly pleasure — but all as if in a nightmare, a decree that could not be changed and against which one could not rebel.

Later, they found themselves walking again between the hedge and bramble along the narrow path. Gina hung on Cici's arm, one hand cupped between his broad, callused palms. From time to time he bent and touched his ardent lips to the back of this hand, slender and smooth as velvet, with piety, as if it were a holy object. He would give his life for her, for the precious creature who was walking beside him. He had never wished for such joy, nor could he even have imagined it in a dream. How could he prove to her that his life was given to her, and that it was hers to do with as she pleased? A fleeting thought flashed through his mind: whether he should throw himself into the water in front of her.

But Gina walked silently beside him, lurching as if sick with wine. Something strange and terrible had pierced her life, something irreversible that would now remain in her forever. Everything else from this point on would lose significance in comparison to it. But could anyone be responsible for it but herself? It was nothing but a hidden side of her being, hidden even to herself, that all of a sudden was revealed by external circumstances. It wasn't merely the event that was important here, for it would be possible to erase it or cancel it by forgetting. But the fact that she was capable of this for no reason, simply because the evening was beautiful, the path quiet, and a man had happened to be beside her — it was enough to drive one mad. And she didn't even have the right to be upset with the man next to her, and vent her anger. Why? Why should he have let this opportunity slip? After all, he did love her. No, there was no one to blame but herself: what foolishness on her part, what stupidity, and how pointless! She could spit into her own face!

She freed herself so abruptly from his arm that he

stopped in his path and turned his wondering face to her. They were approaching the shore now, the first houses of the village, with the darkness thinning. They weren't far away from the guesthouse. In a tone that brooked absolutely no argument, she ordered: 'Now leave me! I'm going alone from here.' Hurriedly, she pulled her hand away as he bent to kiss her. She left him stunned, and disappeared with rapid footsteps, as if running away, without turning her head back.

Barth was already home, preparing to go to sleep. It was clear he had come in only a few minutes before her. It was about half-past twelve. The hoarse strains of the gramophone still burst from Stefano's roof, and occasionally a loud, licentious laugh, which Gina recognised as Latzi's. She was surprised, though, since only a moment ago, as she was passing Stefano's house, she had no sense of the music or the clamour of his guests. But it really didn't matter to her. She took off her dress and slip and stood over the basin by the door to wash herself with cold water. She scrubbed her body, brown from the sun, with a large rust-coloured sponge. The outline of her bathing suit marked her body like a pale white tattoo. She scrubbed with a certain anger, as though to scour some unseen stain. She didn't say a word.

Barth undressed while smoking a cigarette. Then, cautiously, he climbed on the bed, stood to his full height, and slapped the wall where it joined the ceiling. 'Damn!' he said to himself. 'Got away!' Lean, erect, he stood on the bed and scanned the emptiness of the room. No, the mosquito had slipped away. After the lights were turned out, and he was on the verge of sleep, the shrill, vengeful whine would be heard very close to the ear, the bite jarring him into angry wakefulness. He resigned himself to this — there was no other choice. He climbed down from the bed and approached Gina as she was drying herself. He put his arm around her waist.

'Why so quiet, little Gin?'

Gina didn't answer. After a moment: 'How is she?'

'Her fever went up again. I stopped by the café,' he added. 'I thought I'd find you there.'

'I went earlier, but got bored and went for a walk. Were you there all along?'

'Of course not. I left at ten and wandered around the streets.'

'And why didn't you come to the café earlier?' she added with suppressed anger.

'Earlier? I didn't want to interrupt,' he joked, 'as you were in the company of a suitor.'

Gina slid her blue nightgown over her head. With a hint of contempt, she thought bitterly to herself: *Yes, yes, my friend, in the company of a suitor.* As she came up to the bed she said, 'It would have been better if you had disturbed us.'

And she lay down.

Her unusual tone of voice escaped Barth. He poured himself a glass of water and emptied it in a single gulp. He asked if she wanted to read a bit. No, she didn't want to read. He turned out the light and opened the door to the balcony. The sound of voices and laughter rushed into the room at once, louder, clearer, as if from the balcony itself. Through the sounds the tail end of Jejette's shrill laugh could be heard: truncated, grating, with an annoyingly immature impudence. An image of Jejette, full-bosomed, flashed in front of Gina; and an unpleasant sensation rose in her. She lay on her back, close to the wall, her two hands away from her body, this body that seemed strange to her, and to which her intimate attachment was cut. This body of hers was different now, incomprehensible, not the same as yesterday. It aroused fear and nausea in her. An alien and despicable element had just been revealed. Unknown to her thus far, it had been dormant, but ready to subjugate her at any time. She lay motionless, afraid to move lest she touch this body, silent and heavy. If only she could vomit. Simply. Maybe then she could relieve her disgust. She was grateful to Barth for lingering on the balcony. He leaned against the railing, his head turned towards Stefano's roof. She could make out his dark silhouette. If only he would remain standing like this forever! She could not bear his closeness now, his touch, as she could not bear her own. 'Ah! You son of a bitch! Ha-ha-ha!' Stefano's drunken roar could be heard, exultant. It was followed by a moment of silence, during which a straining ear could make out the delicate lapping of the sea as it slapped the shore. Gina's body burned feverishly. She pushed away the sheet that covered her. If only it were possible to sleep, and forget everything for a few hours! But there was no hope that she would soon fall asleep.

Barth entered the room and lay down beside her.

Quietly she rolled to the wall so as not to arouse his attention. But he moved his body close to her, pressing against the full length of her body, his lips seeking hers in the darkness. 'You're not sleeping, Gin my dear.'

Gina recoiled, then sat up. 'Oh, it's unbearably warm … why don't we go for a breath of fresh air, or up to Stefano's?'

'Now? At this hour?'

'So what? I must … if not I'll toss awake until morning. I feel it. If you're too tired, I'll go alone.'

'Perhaps not … Try washing with cold water again.'

Gina jumped out of bed.

'Of course I won't let you go alone at this hour.'

On Stefano's roof, it wasn't yet late at all. Jubilant spirits prevailed. The Japanese fellow and the interpreter stood entangled in each other's arms between two rows of tables that ran along the length of the roof. Marionette-like, they offered each other loud, ringing kisses while Jejette stood by with her two clenched fists planted on her hips, resembling an hourglass. She laughed and followed them with her eyes, like a referee on a playing field. Latzi bowed to the Japanese fellow's companion and struck his fist to his chest, exclaiming in a husky voice: 'Me! Believe me, madame, no one else but me!' then sank back, exhausted, onto a chair, covering his face with both hands. Suzi sat in a chair like a shapeless bundle, laughing silently to herself, not looking at anyone.

'Here they are! You son of a bitch! Ha-ha-ha!' Stefano greeted them. 'Jejette!'

The wrestlers separated and set their dim-witted eyes on the two guests.

Gina drank cognac, one glass, then another. That beastly event still lurked in a corner of her soul, ready to pounce and ambush her. She ordered another drink. 'No, I can't right now,' she answered the interpreter curtly when he asked her to dance. He turned around, bumping into Jejette, and planted a loud, sucking kiss on her mouth, to everyone's amusement.

'What? My girl! Son of a … My daughter, a young girl! I'll show you!' Stefano cried.

Latzi jumped between them. 'Stop! Don't you understand a joke? Here, we are your guests!'

'Ah, you're right, ha-ha-ha! Guests! Jejette, shame on you! Two bottles of rosé! Two! It's on me!'

Gina declined the invitation to join the group. She remained seated. The cognac had eased the gnawing in her heart, but a feeling of sadness had settled in her, and a yearning for another place, undefined, different, and far from here. Mechanically she pulled her lipstick and mirror from her handbag and applied some colour to her lips. The moon hung overhead, suspended as if from nothing. A dull breeze, saturated with the vapours of drunkenness, enveloped this roof, though it seemed incompatible with the purity overhead and the moon's fragile smile.

Barth sat sullenly, legs crossed, waiting for Gina to rise. He didn't drink much. He didn't like to drink on command, without any inner need. What foul spirit had possessed her suddenly? What kind of woman rose at midnight, got dressed, and dashed over to drink cognac at Stefano's? And among such drunk and despicable people whom he knew she could not bear! Who could fathom a woman's heart? This behaviour — one should add it to a list of woman's deeds that apparently were not defined by the laws of cause and effect and that no logic could analyse ... Barth turned and watched Gina sitting motionlessly, staring towards the boisterous group nearby. She didn't look at them, but rather gazed through them, tight-lipped as though holding back some bit of speech so that it wouldn't escape. His heart soured. Despite the arrogance of her profile, there was something afflicted in her sitting as she was. It called to mind another night, on a bench, by a streetlight in the city park. They had met only recently, and their relationship had not yet developed the stability born of mutual compatibility, nor had they undergone the necessary pruning and trimming of the irregularities of character. It was a tremor straining gingerly inside them, a timid, uncertain joy that flickered like a flame in the wind. Beyond a trellis, the click-clack of the late, empty tram could be heard as it rattled back and forth — an external detail engraved in his memory. After a concert and a stop in a café, they had sat there, in the clear night, on the way to her house. Why was she suddenly given to dark thoughts, strange thoughts, as now, which cast a pall between him and her? She had remained in this self-imposed imprisonment for several days, without noticeably changing her behaviour towards him. He had felt suddenly cast aside, into an empty world, without value.

'Aren't you ready to go back, Gin?'

She recoiled from the touch of his hand and looked at him strangely. She mumbled through an absent, excruciating half-smile, more to herself than to him, 'Yes. I suppose so.'

Kraft parked his car not far from the guesthouse and came out in his bathing suit, ready to swim. The morning was still young, though already anointed with molten sunlight. The calm sea, and the dewy homes and gardens facing it, were covered with a dream-like veil. The fishermen's wives, under broad straw hats, were already busy mending their nets on the shore, clear of bathers. Near them, dark and dirty, half-naked children romped in the gravel. Simple, natural, as it had been for generations, since the ascent of humanity; just so, unaffected by the passage of time. For a moment, he felt very close to the quintessence of existence. An unmuddied joy of life washed over him all at once. Polite and friendly, he greeted the fishermen's wives and went to lie on the gravel. Diagonally opposite him, Madame Stefano was already outside her store. She was hidden beneath wispy hair, and her feet shone white in tattered cloth shoes. Shading her eyes with one hand, she looked along the shore as though searching.

'Mar-ti-no!' she called in a dry, broken voice, which echoed all the way up. 'Mar-ti-no! Come-to-wash!'

Kraft turned his gaze toward Barth and Gina's house. If only a man could express himself over a distance, without language, as though through some wireless soul-to-soul telegram! *Here you are, for example, you want to see her at this moment, yearning with every bone in your body — and she, it seems, not even one nerve of her is moved because of it. She will come, for sure, but in another hour or two, as she normally does. She'll be surprised to find you here. You rushed here, like a released arrow, in vain.*

The scratch of approaching footsteps startled him. With faint hopes, he turned his head. 'You're up early!'

Barth smiled broadly and extended his hand. 'It's been several days since you were last here.'

'What about you? How is Gina?'

'Gina?' Barth sat beside him on the gravel. 'She's been in a terrible mood. Two days already. Maybe you could cheer her up a little.'

'Me? Why don't you undress?'

'I have to go and visit Marcelle first.'

'She's not up yet?'

'Still weak. She has to stay in bed another few days …' Then he added: 'Charming girl, don't you think?'

'Hmm. Yes.'

They smoked in silence. A light northerly wind sent a shiver across the surface of the sea. Barth rose. 'I must go. Will you be here all day?'

'I don't know. We'll see.'

Kraft walked out to his car to get a book, then returned and stretched out close to the water. He hadn't read more than a few pages when Gina appeared. He jumped up and greeted her with unconcealed delight. Gina spread her towel on the gravel and sat down. She reached for the book. 'May I see?' She glanced at its lemon-coloured cover, flipped briefly through the pages, and returned the book to its place. Kraft watched her carefully. Her face seemed to him slightly downcast.

Latzi emerged from the guesthouse equipped with his

paints and a stretched canvas. He greeted them from some distance away and walked towards Bouche-de-Loup. Yet after a few steps, he stopped by Stefano's house and set up his easel.

'I'll probably return to Munich soon.'

'What's the hurry?'

On her back, Gina played with the handle of her umbrella. Her expression was completely relaxed.

'Urgent business.'

'I was sure you didn't have any business. It seems you told me so once.'

'I have a wife.'

'And she can't come here?'

'No, she can't.' He smiled bitterly to himself, and added, 'We are about to divorce.' He reached for a leather cigarette case. After a slight pause: 'Will we see each other again, madame?'

'I don't know. I think not.'

'Pity.' After a moment he repeated, as if to himself, 'Great pity.'

Gina suddenly felt sorry for him, for no apparent reason other than that he seemed so miserable. She gazed at him warmly, soothingly. Then she looked out to the smooth sea at her feet and to a tiny boat that receded to a point on the horizon. Kraft grabbed a handful of gravel and with absent-minded application scattered it. A ship with black sails appeared as though sketched on the azure horizon. 'Here, look!' Gina pointed. 'It looks as if it's risen from the depths of eternal night.' The ship stood motionless and was disappearing in front of them, without moving. The smaller boat also could not be seen now. The sea still lolled silently, smooth and bare.

'This summer ...' he whispered. 'I'll think of it for a long time.' He kept his eyes on her. 'Will you let me write to you sometime?'

'What's the point?'

With resignation he said, 'You're right, actually.'

Kraft was quiet. From the side, he watched her as if to engrave her image deep in his memory. His heart shrivelled at the thought that he would no more see her charming face: her youthful lips exultant with an insatiable thirst for living; her omniscient chin, sharply rounded; her eyes, dark as wine, whose gaze pierced without damaging its recipient; the clear feminine forehead crowned with thick hair, dark-chestnut and wavy. 'Would you like to join me on another trip before I leave?'

'When are you leaving?'

'In about three days.'

'I don't think I'll be able to.'

She sat up. She was hot. They entered and swam shoulder to shoulder in the blue water, cool and rejuvenating. It momentarily washed away any bitterness and poured a simple animal exuberance into them. Nowhere was any soul to be seen. Just the two of them in the breadth of an infinite ocean. They shared an unspoken feeling of mingling with the innocence of nature and its lofty wisdom.

After returning to the shore, Gina smiled at Kraft in a friendly manner. Through her tanned face, a fresh paleness filtered, and her eyes shone, pure and lustrous. They were lying on the coarse gravel again, smoking silently as the sun dried their skin.

Suzi came and stretched out nearby. But Latzi continued to stand and paint by Stefano's store, while Stefano and his brood stood around him in a semicircular array. The summer morning was slowly and silently poured back into the ocean of time, as thousands of mornings before it, a morning embroidered with strands of orange sun, blue sea, green gardens, and transparent silence, as well as secret threads that united, yet didn't unite, this couple.

'The Japanese fellow hasn't been here today yet?' Suzi called.

Gina shook her head.

Kraft rose to say he was returning to Nice. With a slightly bashful smile, he added, 'Sometimes, a man may take his own life, out of the fear of dying.' He bent and kissed her hand. 'Say goodbye to Barth.'

'Won't you stop by another time before you leave?'

'Probably not.'

He went to the car. He honked, two, three times and, without turning his head, was off in the blast of his engine. The cloud of white dust that gathered along the road sank slowly back to the ground.

Towards evening the fishermen were still drifting on the surface of the darkening sea; the aromas of dinner were dissipating from the streets of the village. The broken sound of a trumpet could be heard along the main street. In front of Stefano's, there stood a small, slender man dressed in a threadbare tuxedo, a black tie, and tattered shoes white with dust. He held a short trumpet to his lips. Shuffling on her toes, Madame Bremon walked to the garden gate. 'The Italian and his two daughters,' she exclaimed mockingly.

Gina finished eating a slice of watermelon, cleared the table, and went out to relax on the balcony armchair. Barth sat beside her on a chair. She lay back, deep in reverie. Lately, she hadn't said more to Barth than what day-to-day necessity required. To Barth, she seemed somehow changed. He tried to cast about in his mind for the reason. Time and again he received answers to his questions, but they revealed nothing to him, until he gave up asking. Yet, he consoled himself, in time her sullen mood would leave her and all would be restored to normal.

Madame Bremon took a chair from the room and sat with them, her arms crossed. 'Oh! I'm so tired. All day in the boiling sun!' Her hair, peppered with grey, was still thick and curly. It was gathered at the back of her neck in a bun the size of a fist. Bright eyes and a pleasant smile animated her wrinkled face.

She was free for a leisurely chat. 'Next week my daughter will return from the mountains. She'll look after Didi herself.'

Her sons were already married, except for one, who had joined the army and remembered her with an occasional postcard from Indochina. The rest of her children had settled in Saint-Laurent-sur-Ar, six kilometres from here. And herself? As long as she still had strength, she would never make herself a burden to anyone! Above all, she liked to stand on her own two feet. She had always earned a living with her own hands. Years ago, when she was still living with her husband, she had sold flowers. Early every morning she would deliver flowers to Nice, Monaco, and Monte Carlo, because her husband, 'you should know, never lifted a finger'. He was always lazy. He would wake up in the morning, pick up his rifle, and go hunting. Hunting was his passion. He would wander around all day, devil knows where, and return for his soup in the evening. Once in a while, he brought home a jackrabbit or hare, though usually he brought nothing at all. When he finished his meal, he would light up his pipe and while away the evening in a bar. All the worries were hers alone. When the babies had grown, she said to him, 'That's it, my friend! Either you go to work, or we separate!' And then she moved here.

And her husband? He went hunting, as before, and became a burden on her eldest son, the one who had visited her on Sunday with his children. Maybe they thought he was a weak man? If only they had seen him! Big and strong! They'd think he was thirty-five, no more! Unlike her, whose life of drudgery had prematurely aged her body. What could be expected, with five children! Feeding them, raising them, marrying them off, and all by a widow … for it really was as though she were a widow.

'And your daughter married Monsieur Larouette after you moved here?' Barth enquired.

No, she had married before. Ten years ago. She was nineteen at the time. Madame Bremon had objected at first, even though Monsieur Larouette was wealthy. 'The old hag owns everything, you should know. The house they live in and its huge garden. The house next door, rented to the Japanese man on the first floor. All hers, along with huge tracts of land and the vineyard. And apart from that, plenty of cash in the banks. And being an only child, it is all his to inherit. And he has a good position, too, in the wine-and-oil firm.' So why did she object to the match? Because of that stingy and shifty old hag. It was well known in this area, certainly within a one-hundred-kilometre radius. They, members of the Bremon family, were poor, but they knew how to behave. They knew what was decent and proper. After all, there was a limit to miserliness! But her daughter insisted. She wanted only him. The children loved each other. Finally, she gave her permission. And she wasn't sorry. Her daughter was happy with him. He adored her; she was the apple of his eye. He even treated Madame Bremon with great respect. And the relations between them were friendly. They could plainly see! He provided her with wine and oil the year around, though she didn't need any, thank God! For years she had done the washing for the guesthouse, and she had all that she needed, but it was a sign of dedication on his part. As she always said: a man who loves his wife loves his mother-in-law.

And his mother? She was better off not seeing her! She was very careful not to run across her, but she always sent for her, for one errand or another. 'Have you ever seen such a stinking creature? She weighs over a hundred kilos and never budges!'

'But must you go when she calls for you?'

'Must? Of course not! No one can force me. But I don't want to get on her bad side: it's hell! She might make up the worst lies and make your name dirt, you have no idea what that woman is capable of, the old hag! I want peace. There was a time when we didn't even exchange greetings, for two whole years. Then, once she sent for me and I went. What do you expect? My own daughter lives in her house, after all. I can't lock myself out forever! But I'll avoid her door if I can help it.'

The balcony was already dark. Gina rose.

'Are we going out for a bit?'

As they passed Stefano's, the storekeeper called from the door. 'Aren't you coming up? We have a show today.'

There was no way out.

There were about two dozen townsmen at the tables, some of them with their wives. Stefano, his sleeves rolled up, was having a drink with one group, laughing and roaring in his coarse voice. Jejette was serving.

The Italian in the tuxedo was trying hard to tune his violin, letting out stray, solitary notes. Two girls, aged eight and ten, sat motionlessly at a nearby table, wearing short, bell-shaped pink dresses. Pink ribbons, tied like huge butterflies, were knotted in their wispy hair. Their scrawny legs were clad in knee socks, once white, and sandals coated with yesterday's mud and dust. Sunk in blatant poverty, they sat courteously, with forced seriousness, waiting their turn and looking blankly ahead. Overhead, musty stars were beginning to flicker.

Gina and Barth chose the furthest table, close to the door. Cici appeared immediately. He shook the Italian's hand and approached them. 'I saw you coming up.'

Gina's face darkened momentarily.

'You know him?' enquired Barth.

Cici sat down. 'He has a wife with tuberculosis and nine children, each smaller than the next. They came from Italy eight months ago. He looked for a long time but couldn't find a job. Now he goes from door to door with his daughters and brings home a few pennies. If you could only see the shack they live in! Not fit for a dog.'

The Italian began to play the violin, his girls standing close by, stiff as rods, singing an Italian children's song in thin, timorous voices. The song and accompaniment were so pathetically ridiculous, so painfully incompetent, that Gina and Barth averted their eyes in embarrassment. It was a caricature that stirred up disgust and nausea. Never before had they heard anything like it. Afterwards, the girls passed around a small bowl. Then the father began a solo from *Carmen*, his face cast like a wax mask, motionless and lacking any expression. No, Barth would never again go to the opera to hear *Carmen*! After that, the two girls sang a duet, their father conducting them with his outstretched finger.

The Japanese fellow arrived with his girlfriend. Stefano called to them, waving his hand. One of the girls passed around the collection dish once again. She then took off her pink dress, stripping down to flesh-coloured under-wear. She lifted a small box from under a table. It was open at both ends. She placed it on a faded red carpet that her father had unrolled on the floor. Bending and twisting her head through her legs, she wriggled back and forth through the open box. Stefano clapped his hands, roaring with laughter. She squeezed herself into the box again, this time with her sister rolling her to and fro across the carpet, their father supervising the performance. At the end of this number, there was an intermission. The Italian ordered coffee for his daughters. They drank it reluctantly, tired, pale, and sleepy.

When Barth turned to the next table and got involved in a conversation with the Japanese fellow and his friend, Cici seized the opportunity to whisper: 'It's been a few days. I haven't been able to speak with you. You're avoiding me.'

'You are mistaken. I have nothing to discuss with you.'

'But, that night ...' Cici whispered passionately.

'What? Don't you dare, do you hear!' Her face turned red. She trembled with restrained fury.

'But this is not a game, madame,' and then he added, conciliatory: 'If only you knew what's in my heart!'

'Enough! I don't want to hear anything. Not even another word.'

Cici turned pale. Through his teeth he hissed: 'I'm not a toy, madame! I don't let anyone use me as they need me and throw me away afterwards. You watch out!'

'Ha!' She laughed in his face. 'You have spoken to me for the last time!' She turned her face away from him.

Mechanically he began to fidget with his empty glass. Pale, thin-lipped, his broad mouth sealed as though with nails. He parted his lips slightly and, through the crack, his even teeth sparkled white.

At that moment, Stefano's drunken roar could be heard

above the clamour of the guests: 'That's enough! I won't allow any more of this! You son of a bitch!'

All heads were instantly turned towards him. He stood opposite the startled Italian, whose violin already rested on his shoulder, ready to play, and thundered: 'The concert is over! I won't allow it! *Finito!*'

Cici rose and marched heavily, pale and square, and stood before Stefano. Suddenly there was silence. The starry night was cool on the roof tonight, and breathless. Cici said quietly, ominously: 'Let them finish! Let them earn their living!'

'What? A beggar? A bum? Are you giving me orders in my house?' And he landed a dull, heavy blow on Cici's head.

In an instant, a knife flashed. Stefano clutched his left side with both hands. A dark spot was spreading across his light shirt. As he fell to the floor, he screamed, 'He killed me! He murdered me! Son of a —'

Cici bolted through the cluster of tables and disappeared. The voice of a woman broke into a whimper. Jejette screamed.

Barth and Gina took advantage of the confusion and slipped downstairs. When they turned into their house's garden after an hour's walk, a figure, veiled in shadow, emerged from a wall and came towards them. Cici put a finger to his lips, signifying silence, and whispered, 'I just wanted to say goodbye. I'm escaping tonight.'

Gina extended her hand, and he kissed it. Then, silently, he pressed Barth's hand, and slipped away.

'Why, for God's sake? Isn't there any other way?'

Barth sat on the edge of the bed, his feet dangling above the floor. He held his head in his two hands and remained frozen for a while. The evening twilight filtered quietly through the doorway to the balcony, mingled with vague, distant, and isolated cries. A gentle breeze blew from time to time. Beyond the few treetops in front of the balcony, the sea could be seen, a shudder racing across its surface.

Gina took a bundle of dresses from the closet and placed them over a chair. Two leather suitcases lay open on the floor.

Barth lifted his head again and followed her deliberate movements. He had a feeling he would never see her again. In one fell swoop, everything was suddenly un-important, superfluous. For him now, there was no reason to go back to Paris, only to get up early each morning to get to work on time at the office — no reason to work, or to rest.

'This emotional crisis ... is there no other way to over-come it?'

He felt his words were in vain, and that no earthly power could prevent her from enacting her decision. Nevertheless, he continued to speak, if only from the in-tensity of his desperation.

'If you must be alone for a time, it could be arranged so that no one would suffer ... We could rent a room in Paris. Is it because of Marcelle?'

She stopped packing for a moment, and stared at him. 'Marcelle? Nonsense. Of course not.'

'I know.'

And after a second: 'None of this is about you, Barth. My feelings for you haven't changed.'

'Then why this? Why? What happened suddenly? Don't you have any faith in me?'

'Do you want me to lie to you? I have never lied to you. Do you think that I know why? I can't even explain this to myself, except that it's me … just me. I feel we must end it. There is no other choice. All week, I've been struggling with this feeling.'

She continued folding her dresses, packing them meticulously in the suitcases, one after the other. The room's void was filled with a strange feeling. The fondness that he had developed over the past weeks to these four walls, to the furniture, to every detail of this room, vanished at once, as if it had never been. Gina herself, who stood packing her bags with clothes and things — even she was now a stranger. There was no longer any bridge that led him to her.

As if thinking aloud, Barth spoke, in a warm voice, seething with an ocean of sadness: 'Didn't I sense these last days that something was about to happen? Every minute was filled with that certainty. And you? You were silent. As though I didn't deserve being spoken to. The two of us together, maybe we could have found a solution. I knew you were suffering. If only we had examined the reason together, openly, perhaps it could have been erased.'

Outside, it was darkening. Shadows had begun gathering in the corners of the room. Not far away, someone's loud laughter could be heard intermittently. 'It's not

Latzi,' Barth said trivially. He sat frozen in the same position, a sickly fever infiltrating his bowels. He could feel his rapid, agitated heartbeat.

She closed the balcony door and switched on the light. As she passed him, she slipped her hand through his tousled hair, towards the nape of his neck. Then she continued packing. Something heavy spread through the room, making the air dense and unfit to breathe.

'And why must it be tomorrow, Gina? Couldn't you wait a few more days?'

'You're tearing my heart.'

'And you yourself? Look, Gin, think it over again. You love the sea. We'll finish our time here, then you can see. Maybe you're afraid your resolve will weaken meanwhile? If it does — then your decision is unnecessary! It can't just be possible to destroy the lives of two people like this — on a whim!'

Gina stood very erect, not doing anything, her arms hanging limply at her sides. Her eyes shone feverishly, seeming larger, encircled by dark rings. Her lips looked somehow used now. 'I didn't say I wouldn't come back.'

'I might come back,' she repeated more for herself than for him. She stooped over her suitcases again.

'If only I knew it would last a month, three months, half a year!' He rose and walked to the balcony door. Standing there, he faced the room. Silently, he followed her movements. From outside, the muffled sounds of a piano could be heard, probably from a nearby guesthouse. And this music, too, was no longer familiar, a part of the string of luminous days and nights coloured by sun and moon.

On the contrary, it was alienating, annoying; a strange element that did not belong here. Certainly now was not the time for an evening's light and pleasant melancholy to spill into the soul unconsciously, and to spread as the distant, diffuse scent of violets. Now, in this void, lay the scattered fragments of something irreversibly shattered, neither his nor Gina's fault, but rather by the cruelty of fate — something orphaned, gnawing, and piercing to tears. The six weeks they had spent here had been a time to mould bright, fresh memories. It had become clear to them both that the time hadn't all been entirely pleasant; on the contrary, it had been filthy, in the stupefying heat, plagued with mosquitoes, even boredom, yes, simple bore-dom, and that it would leave them bitter because of its ending, which might cast its shadow backwards. This place had robbed him of Gina without his knowing why. And now, there was no recourse.

He stood leaning against the door, his eyes set on Gina with a hollow and unseeing gaze. After she shut one of the suitcases, she stretched and then sat down in a chair. She would do the rest early tomorrow. She was tired.

He sat beside her. He took her hand and stroked it. Not a sound entered from outside now. Silence enveloped them. Had it not been for the two suitcases in the centre of the room declaring the certain ruin of a stable, regular life, one might think that nothing had changed, that this evening's tranquillity mingling with two silent people was no different in the least from similar evenings that had preceded it in this room or in another.

As he wrapped his arm around her waist to draw her

closer, he sensed her slight resistance. He let her go.

'Let's go out for a bit.'

He rose without a word.

In the café near the Japanese house, they sat alone on the covered veranda, dark and mosquito-ridden, whose screen walls were covered with climbing tendrils that bore bunches of green, unripe berries. Barth was drinking a mixture of wine and cognac, his face increasingly flushed. He didn't speak. From time to time he glanced at Gina, who sat opposite him, opening his mouth as if to speak, though he didn't say a word.

'Shall we ruin this evening with drunkenness?' she said.

He set glassy eyes on her, his face a strangely tragic mask. After a moment, he replied hoarsely, 'I had no idea you could be so cruel.' Suddenly, as if to himself, he added, 'Maybe there is another man here ...'

'Why the probing? If that were so, would I have kept it from you? In spite of everything, I regard you as a true friend. Maybe someday I'll be able to talk about it. When I understand myself better ... If I could say anything now it would certainly come out coarse, and false. One's deeds — they can't always be explained. Let me first try to resolve this on my own, for clarity. One thing I can tell you: my respect for my own body has been shaken. The reason? It might be small or insignificant ... but as long as I cannot live with it, I cannot live with you ...'

'Words! Sophistry!' A caustic outburst, unlike him. And in a different voice, pleading: 'Tell me, Gin, do you want me to uproot you from my heart? Yes?'

'I would be very miserable.'

They both remained silent. With his eyes cast down on the table, Barth drank with mute obstinacy.

Marcelle appeared, wearing a woollen sweater, her face sunken and pale through her tan. She smiled slightly, as if ashamed of her apparent weariness. Silently, Barth extended his hand to her, and returned his gaze to the table.

'I'm happy to see you out and about,' Gina said courteously to her.

'I've been out since yesterday.' And with another slight smile, she added: 'I have no intention of succumbing.'

'No. Don't do it. But it might be better to take precautions in the evenings. The night is cool.'

'The worst of it is that the doctor explicitly forbade me to bathe in the sea.'

'You've bathed enough, I would think. Next summer I'm sure you'll be allowed to again.'

'Next summer …'

To Gina, it seemed that Marcelle had matured, had become more of a woman than she had been before her illness. It was as if she had caught a glimpse of the mystery of life and death. All at once she felt closer to her, deeply close, unconditionally. 'I'm leaving here tomorrow.' The words slipped out of her mouth.

'By yourself?'

'By myself,' she said, and added immediately: 'I must travel to my parents in Vienna.'

Barth, like an echo, repeated: 'Yes. Must travel to Vienna. What will you have, Marcelle? Hey, you?' He thrust his voice into the void of the hall. 'A hot glass of milk for Mademoiselle Marcelle!'

'And now it is up to you to amuse him in his widow-hood,' Gina joked.

'I'll do what I can, as long as he agrees to be consoled by me.'

They chatted for a while, idle chat, without Barth's participation. The surrounding silence mingled with the dull murmur of the sea. When Marcelle rose to leave, they accompanied her.

The train would arrive at any moment. They stood silently on the platform. They had nothing to say to each other because they had too much to say to each other. Barth's knees and thighs throbbed with tremendous fatigue as though all strength had been sapped from them. A painful void filled his chest. The train had not yet arrived, but it would not be late, not late. There was no hope for some unexpected mishap — a broken track, for example — that might cause delay. Maybe then she would abandon her journey entirely … Yet on the other hand, Barth hoped it would hurry, if only to hasten the end of the ending. Such waiting was difficult to bear. He poked a cigarette between his lips, forgetting to light it. Passengers, carrying woollen blankets on their arms, were standing next to fancy suitcases and trunks, or pacing back and forth along the platform. The glass foyer was filled with a quiet, stubborn heat. Porters were pushing their metal trolleys laden with piles of luggage. On the third track, a single engine passed with a shriek and a column of thick, opaque smoke. Barth began to pace unconsciously and without direction, then changed his mind and returned to Gina. She leaned against his body and touched her lips to his cheek. She took his hand between her two burning palms and stroked it slowly, silently. Why was life such that a single stone could land and cause such desolation, without one ever knowing from whose hand it had been cast? Who was to blame? Soon, the train would come, and she would journey from here, never to return. Soon, something would be torn irreparably in her heart. And after a time, even if she did return and renew her life, she would still be unable to mend this tear, the tear of the separation that was about to begin in a few minutes. She would never be able to pick up where she had now stopped, at that exact place.

The train approached, like a giant beast with heaving breath. They felt a blast of heat as the engine passed. It lurched to a stop and passengers clamoured to their places. Barth carried the hand luggage. 'It will stop for fifteen minutes. I'll go buy some more fruit.' He disappeared, and returned almost immediately with a paper bag filled with large peaches.

Again they stood on the platform, by the carriage stairs now, not knowing what to say to each other. Barth remembered the cigarette dangling coldly from his lips, and struck a match. Indistinctly, an official announced the garbled names of stops and destinations no one could understand. Gina would pass through all of these jumbled stations during the night, and the train would take her further and further away. It would not be difficult to climb on a train such as this one afternoon, and pass through days and nights and garbled stops to reach her — *but, nevertheless, you will never board and never arrive. From now on you have no emotional possibility to do so.* He set his eyes on her and saw that she was quite pale, and veiled in sadness. Her eyes were sunk in their sockets. He would have screamed to her: 'Why, Gin, why and for what?' But the words died on his lips. Then he clasped her like a wild animal and pressed her to his chest, almost crushing her. He saw tears welling in her eyes, though they never fell. '*En voiture!*' cried the conductor. A whistle shrieked. She pulled herself from his arms and jumped onto the train. 'Don't think badly of me, 'Dolph, and forgive me!'

The train lurched forward. Gina leaned out the open window and waved her handkerchief. For a long while, she could distinguish his figure, standing still, like a lifeless post, head tilted slightly, holding his hat high and motionless.

Paris, 1932